W9-BYK-536

GIVE IT UP!

and other short stories

by
FRANZ KAFKA

illustrated by
PETER KUPER

CONTENTS

INTRODUCTION

By JULES FEIFFER

Kuper? Kafka? Kuper plays Kafka? Do we need this? Kafka? Kuper? The Dream Team? Is this really such a good idea? Especially for those of us who detest the *Classics Illustrated* concept, which is to upgrade the image of comic art by cross-dressing it with culturally significant heavyweights.

Fiction—that is, great fiction—is holy writing. It moves, embraces, endangers, inspires, and, at its most transcendant, works on you like an improved substitute for life. It can, if you listen, alert and change you. The right book at the right age is a better therapist than a shrink.

To 'classically illustrate' Melville, Tolstoy, Dostoyevsky et al doesn't make them accessible, it makes them mute. It subverts the writer's intent, which is to engage in a passionate conspiracy with the reader, a private act that evolves into running dual monologues. In our heads, we talk back to books that talk to us. But add pictures and panels and balloons to the text, and the secret of communion that gives fiction its power is betrayed. The trade-off is T.V. stills. And no one talks back to T.V., except to yell at it.

Kuper, in this volume, doesn't do what I hate, he does what I love. Jazz. This book is a series of riffs, visual improvisations on short takes by the old master. It becomes a diverting, even daring, high wire act, where Kafka's stoic Euro-alienation meets and merges with Kuper's thoroughly American rock and roll alienation. Our alienation is noisier, more raucous than theirs. Americans expect to be winners even as we lose, so we scream. Central Europeans expect to lose, so they shrug. In these pages, Kuper gives us the screaming shrug. And it works. Like Bird doing "Embraceable You," it may not be Gershwin, but it's art. And I, for one, talk back to it.

"A book should serve as the ax for the frozen sea within us."
- Franz Kafka

ISBN 1-56163-125-6
Library of Congress catalog card no. 95-68471
Art © 1995 Peter Kuper
Introduction © 1995 Jules Feiffer
Book design by Peter Kuper
Type design by Ann Decker and Peter Kuper
Additional typesetting by Ying Gu
Thanks to Laird Ogden for assistance
Stories by Franz Kafka adapted by permission of Schocken Books, Inc.
First printing July 1995

5   4   3   2

ComicsLit is an imprint and trademark of

NANTIER · BEALL · MINOUSTCHINE
Publishing inc.
new york

Dedicated to my friend Tony, whose
passion for Kafka was infectious.

A Little Fable.

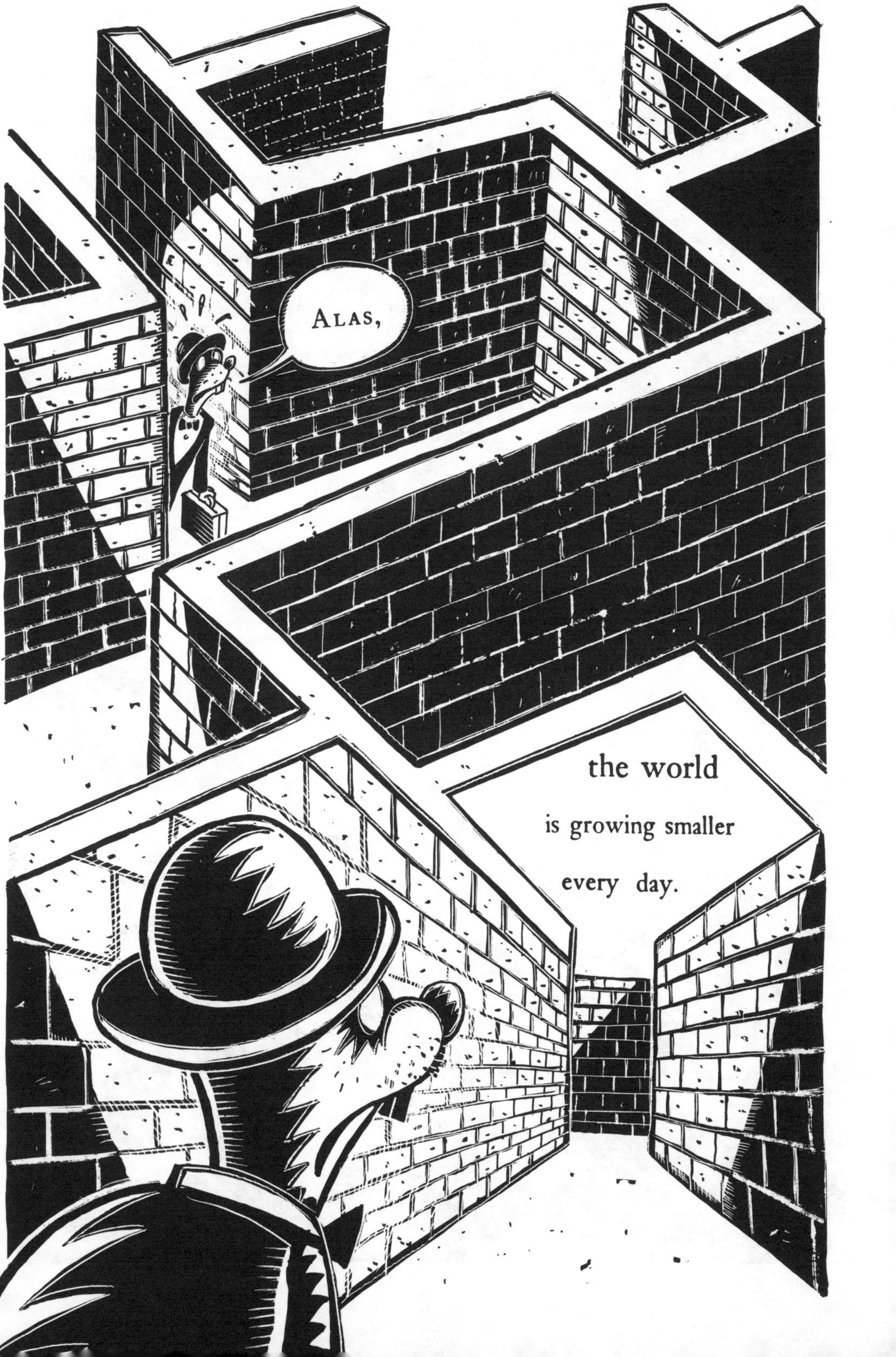
Alas,
the world
is growing smaller
every day.

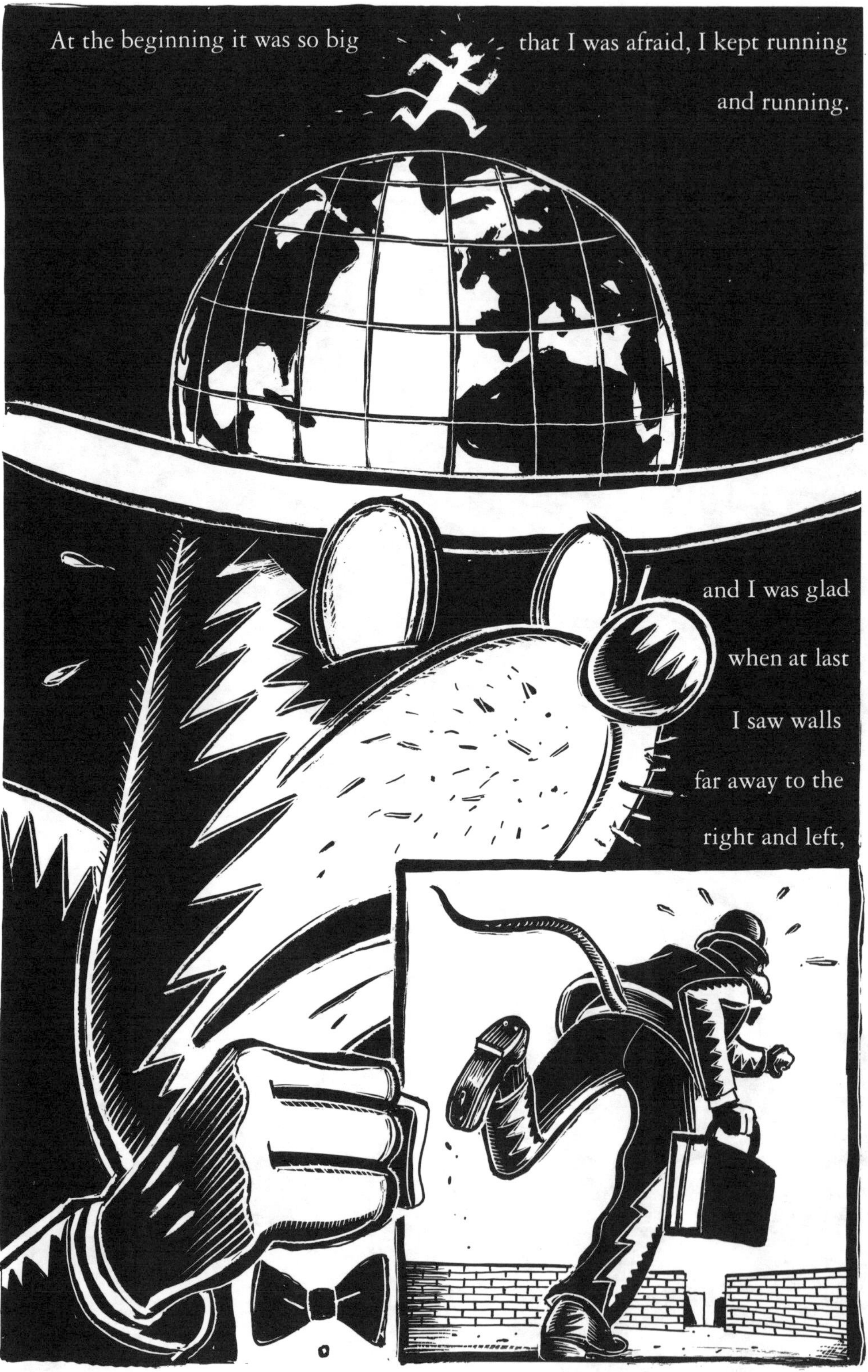
At the beginning it was so big
that I was afraid, I kept running
and running.
and I was glad
when at last
I saw walls
far away to the
right and left,

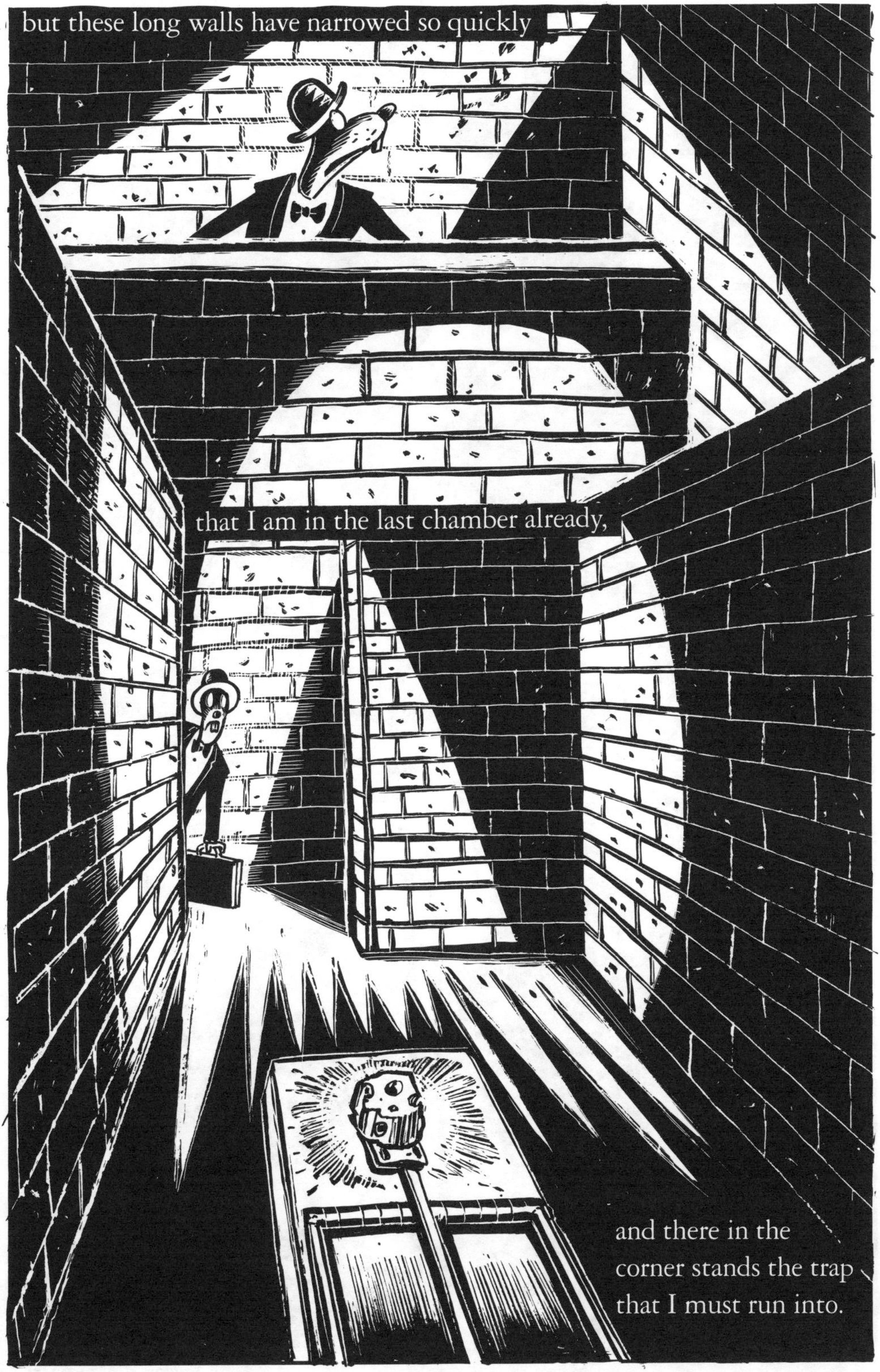
but these long walls have narrowed so quickly
that I am in the last chamber already,
and there in the corner stands the trap that I must run into.

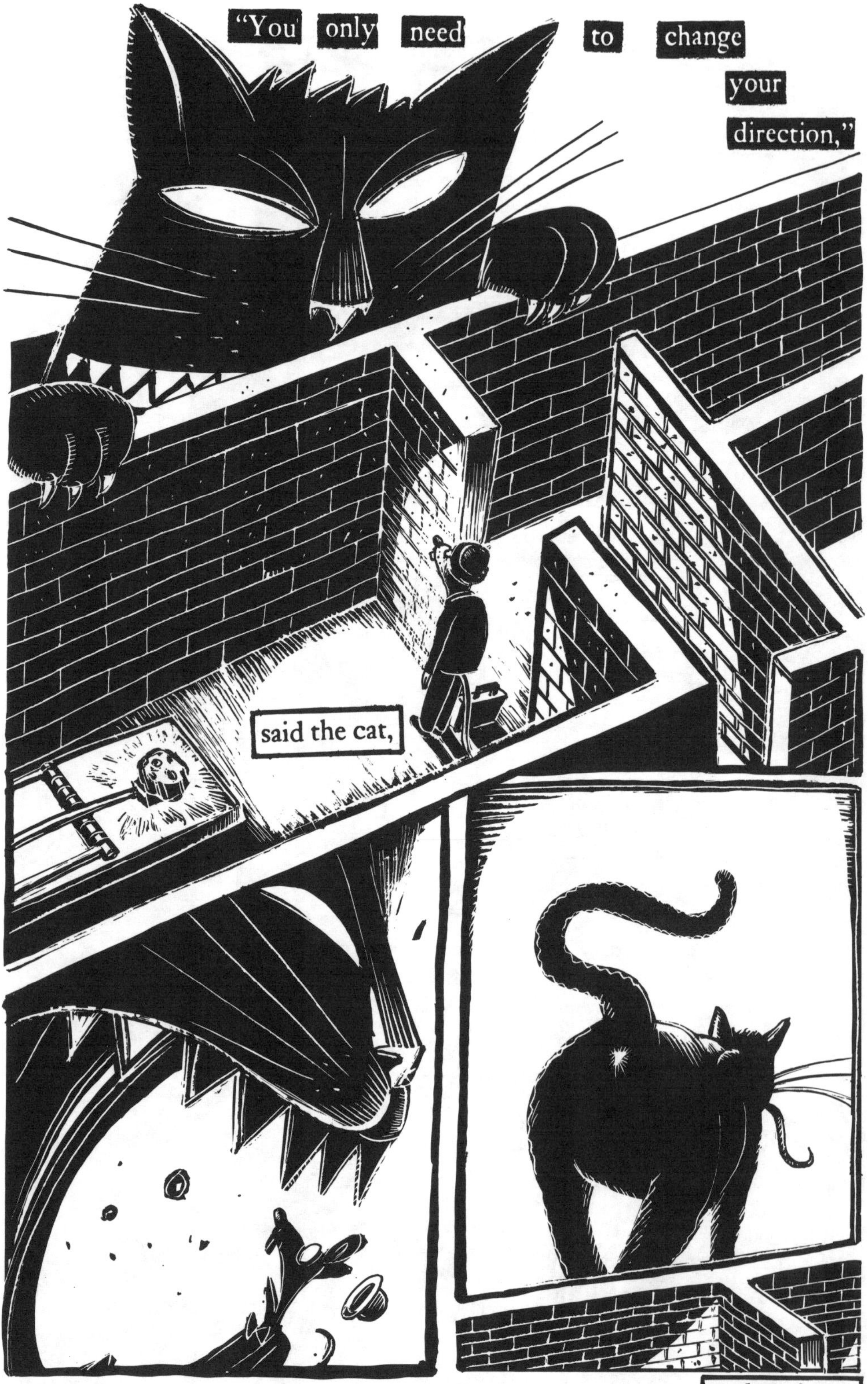
"You only need to change your direction,"
said the cat,
and ate it up.

The Bridge

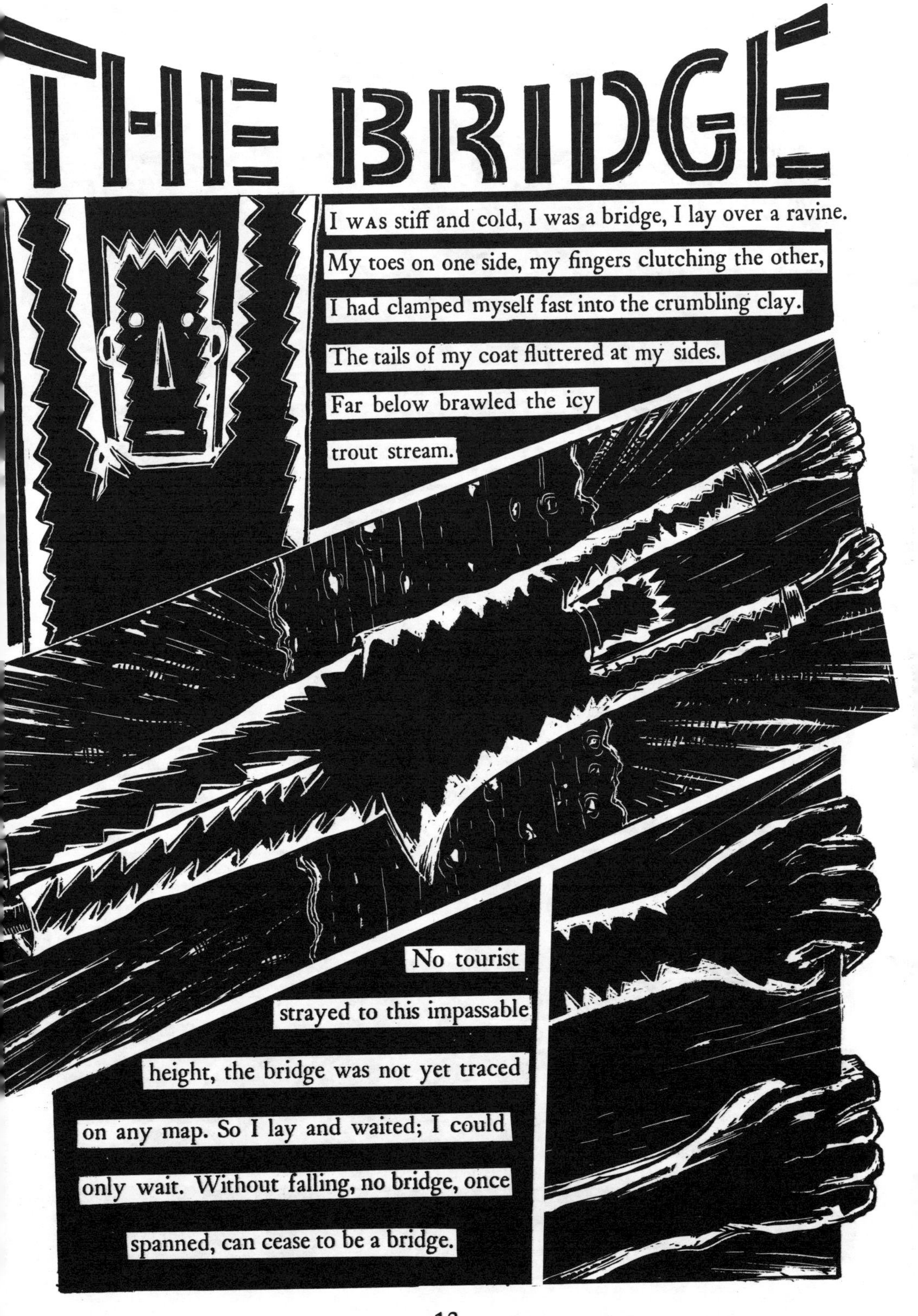
THE BRIDGE
I WAS stiff and cold, I was a bridge, I lay over a ravine.
My toes on one side, my fingers clutching the other,
I had clamped myself fast into the crumbling clay.
The tails of my coat fluttered at my sides.
Far below brawled the icy
trout stream.
No tourist
strayed to this impassable
height, the bridge was not yet traced
on any map. So I lay and waited; I could
only wait. Without falling, no bridge, once
spanned, can cease to be a bridge.

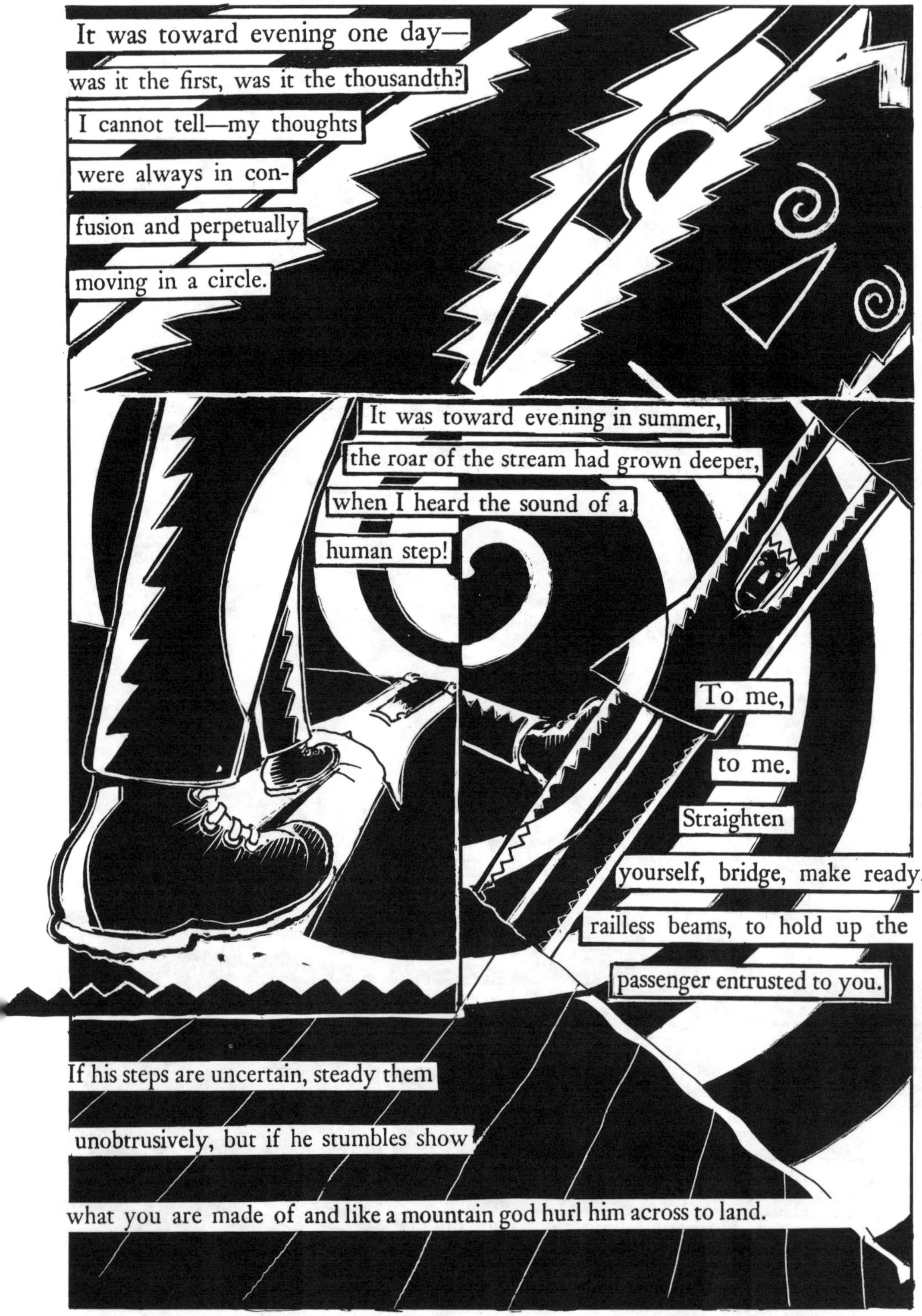
It was toward evening one day—
was it the first, was it the thousandth?
I cannot tell—my thoughts
were always in con-
fusion and perpetually
moving in a circle.
It was toward evening in summer,
the roar of the stream had grown deeper,
when I heard the sound of a
human step!
To me,
to me.
Straighten
yourself, bridge, make ready,
railless beams, to hold up the
passenger entrusted to you.
If his steps are uncertain, steady them
unobtrusively, but if he stumbles show
what you are made of and like a mountain god hurl him across to land.

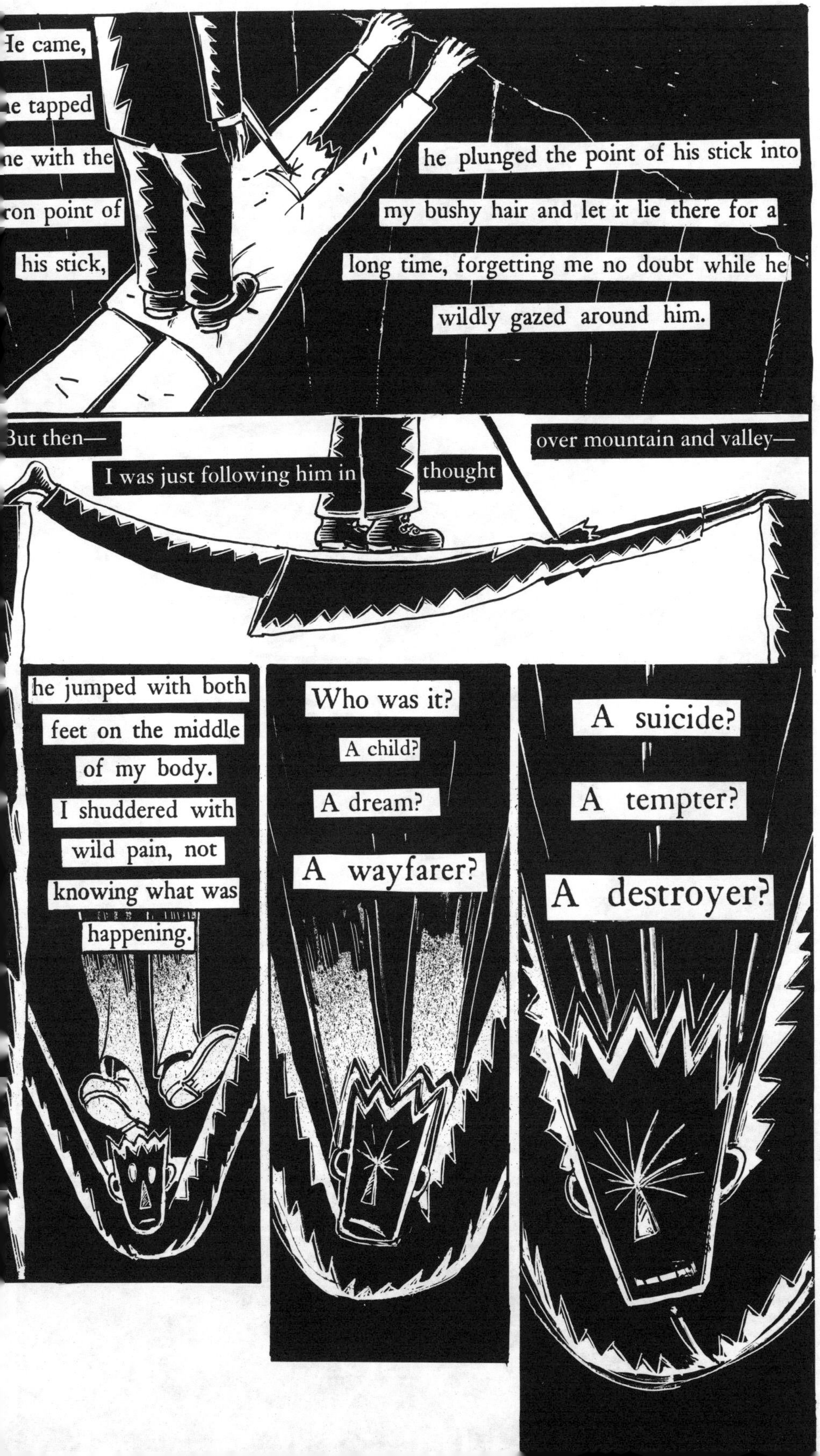

He came,
he tapped
me with the
iron point of
his stick,
he plunged the point of his stick into my bushy hair and let it lie there for a long time, forgetting me no doubt while he wildly gazed around him.
But then—
I was just following him in
thought
over mountain and valley—
he jumped with both feet on the middle of my body. I shuddered with wild pain, not knowing what was happening.
Who was it?
A child?
A dream?
A wayfarer?
A suicide?
A tempter?
A destroyer?

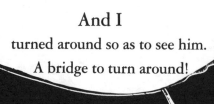

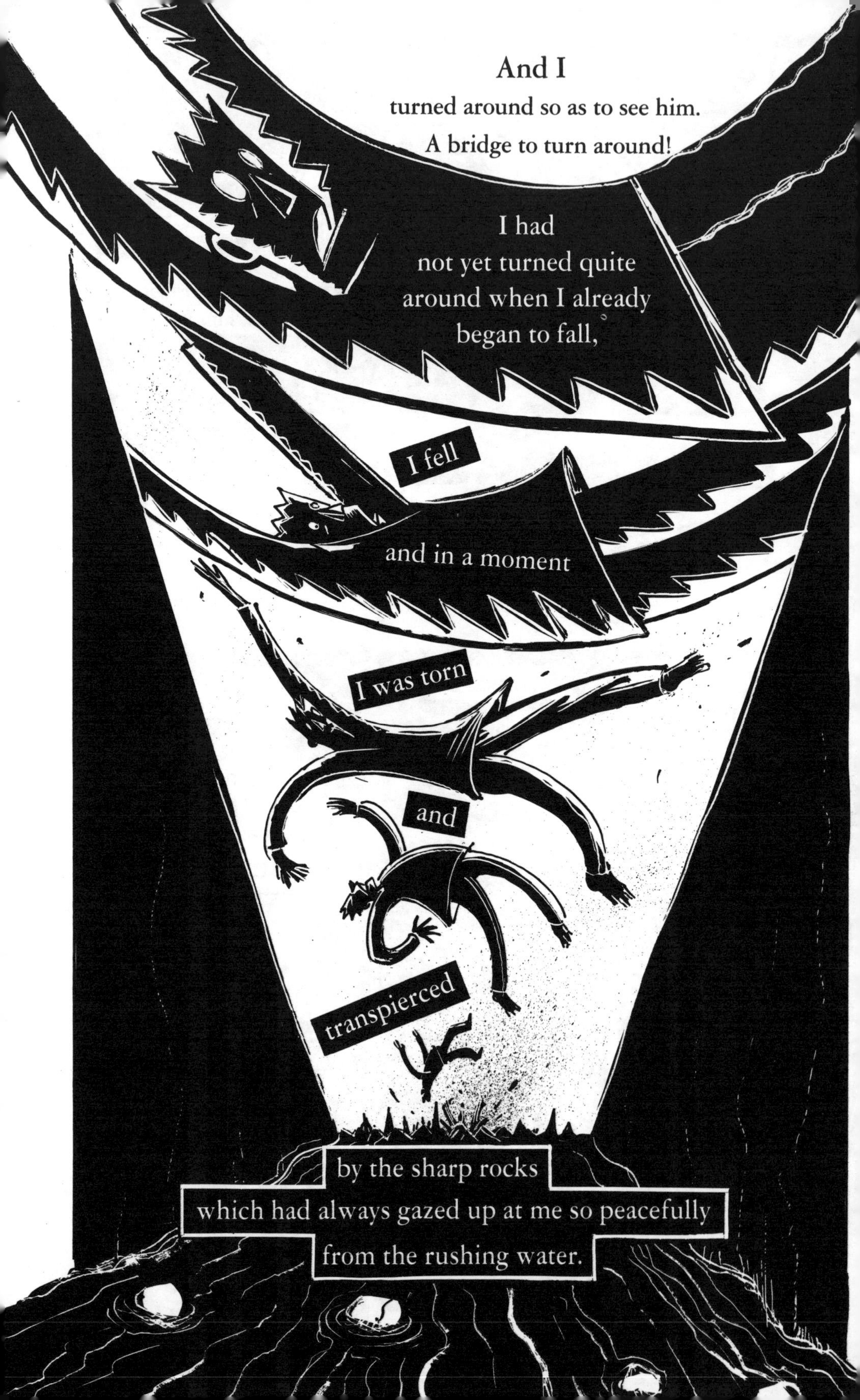

And I
turned around so as to see him.
A bridge to turn around!

I had
not yet turned quite
around when I already
began to fall,

I fell

and in a moment

I was torn

and

transpierced

by the sharp rocks
which had always gazed up at me so peacefully
from the rushing water.

Gíve It Up!

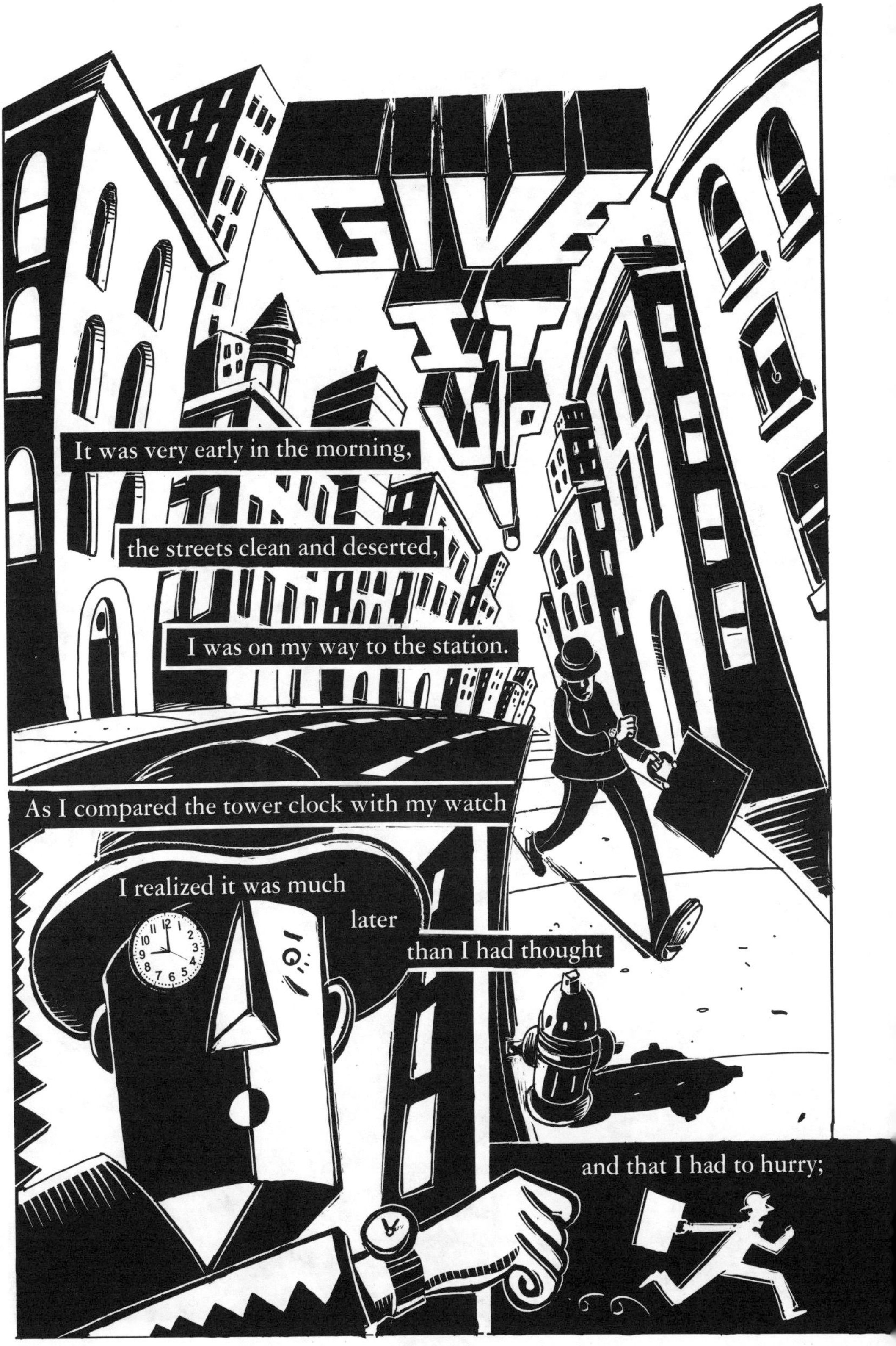
GIVE IT UP!
It was very early in the morning,
the streets clean and deserted,
I was on my way to the station.
As I compared the tower clock with my watch
I realized it was much
later
than I had thought
and that I had to hurry;

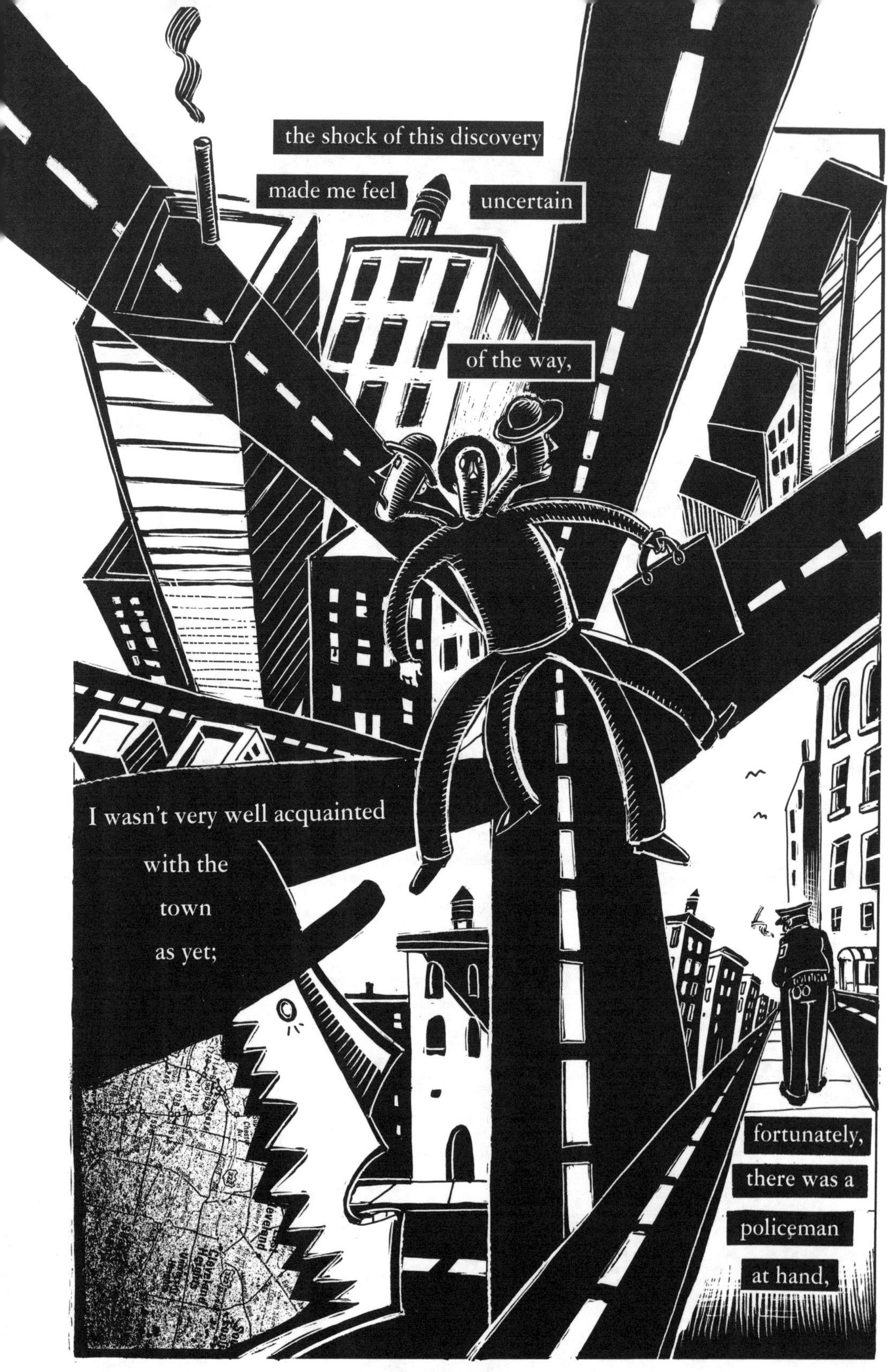
the shock of this discovery
made me feel
uncertain
of the way,
I wasn't very well acquainted
with the
town
as yet;
fortunately,
there was a
policeman
at hand,

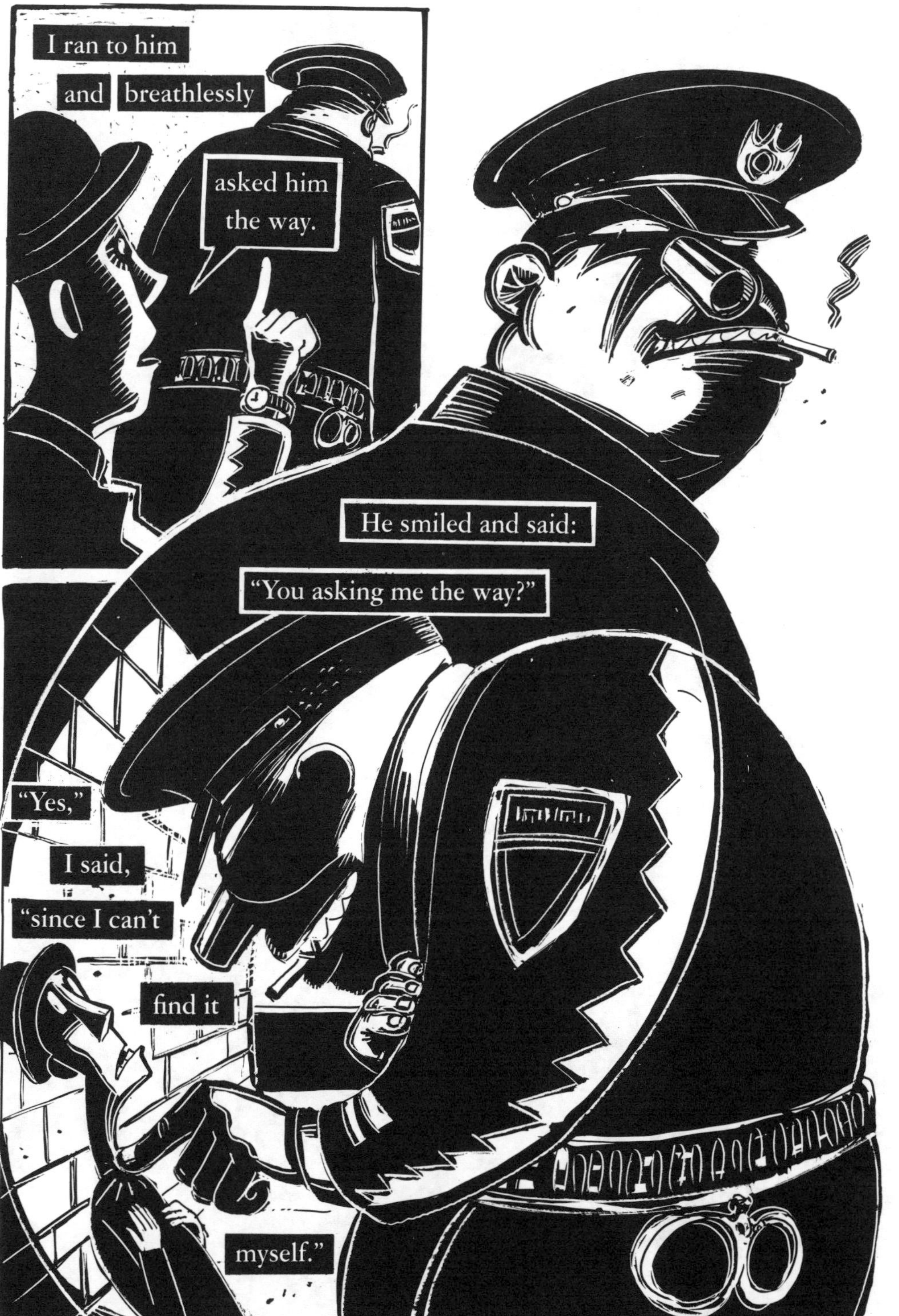
I ran to him
and
breathlessly
asked him the way.
He smiled and said:
"You asking me the way?"
"Yes,"
I said,
"since I can't
find it
myself."

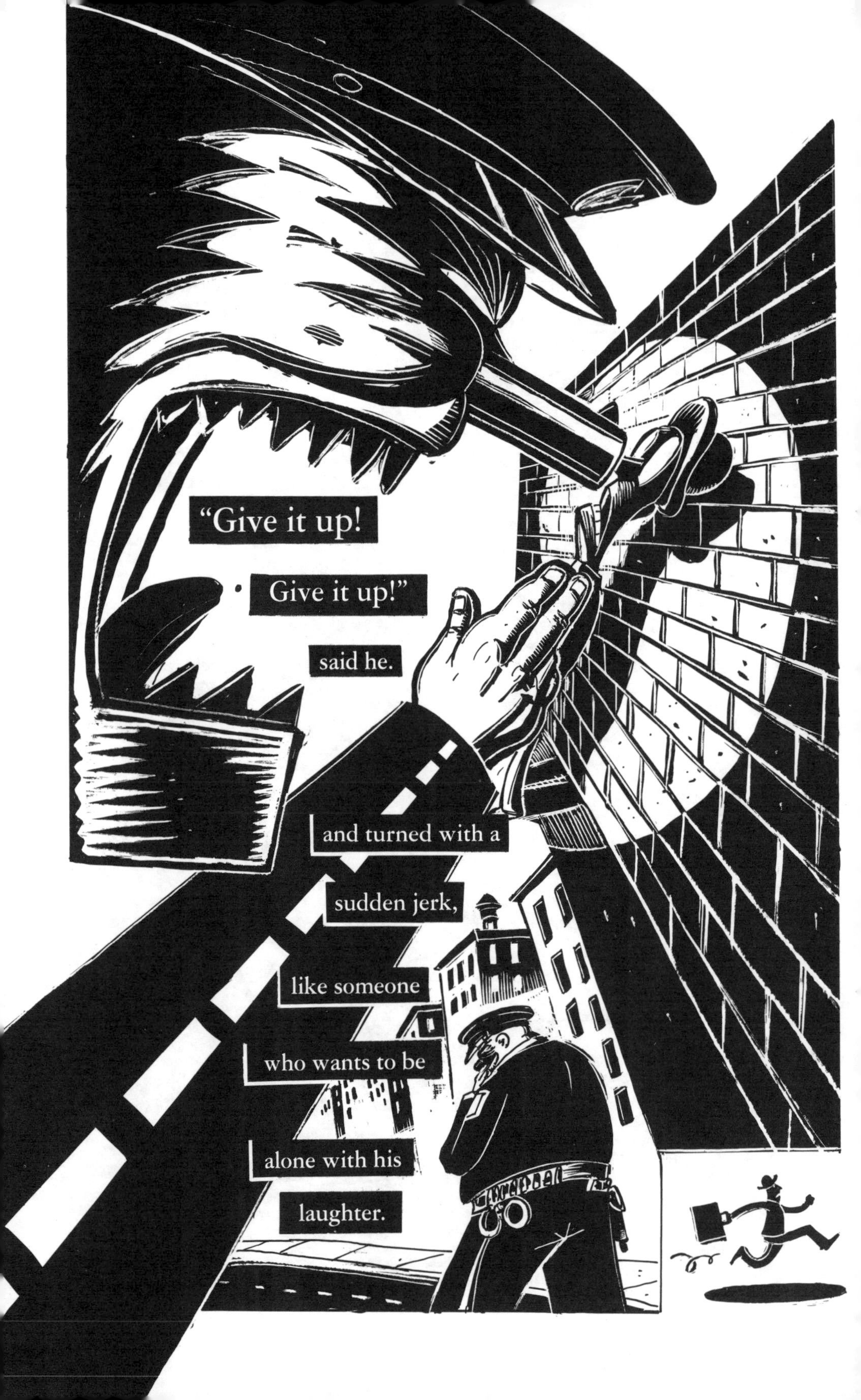
"Give it up!
Give it up!"
said he.
and turned with a
sudden jerk,
like someone
who wants to be
alone with his
laughter.

A Hunger Artist

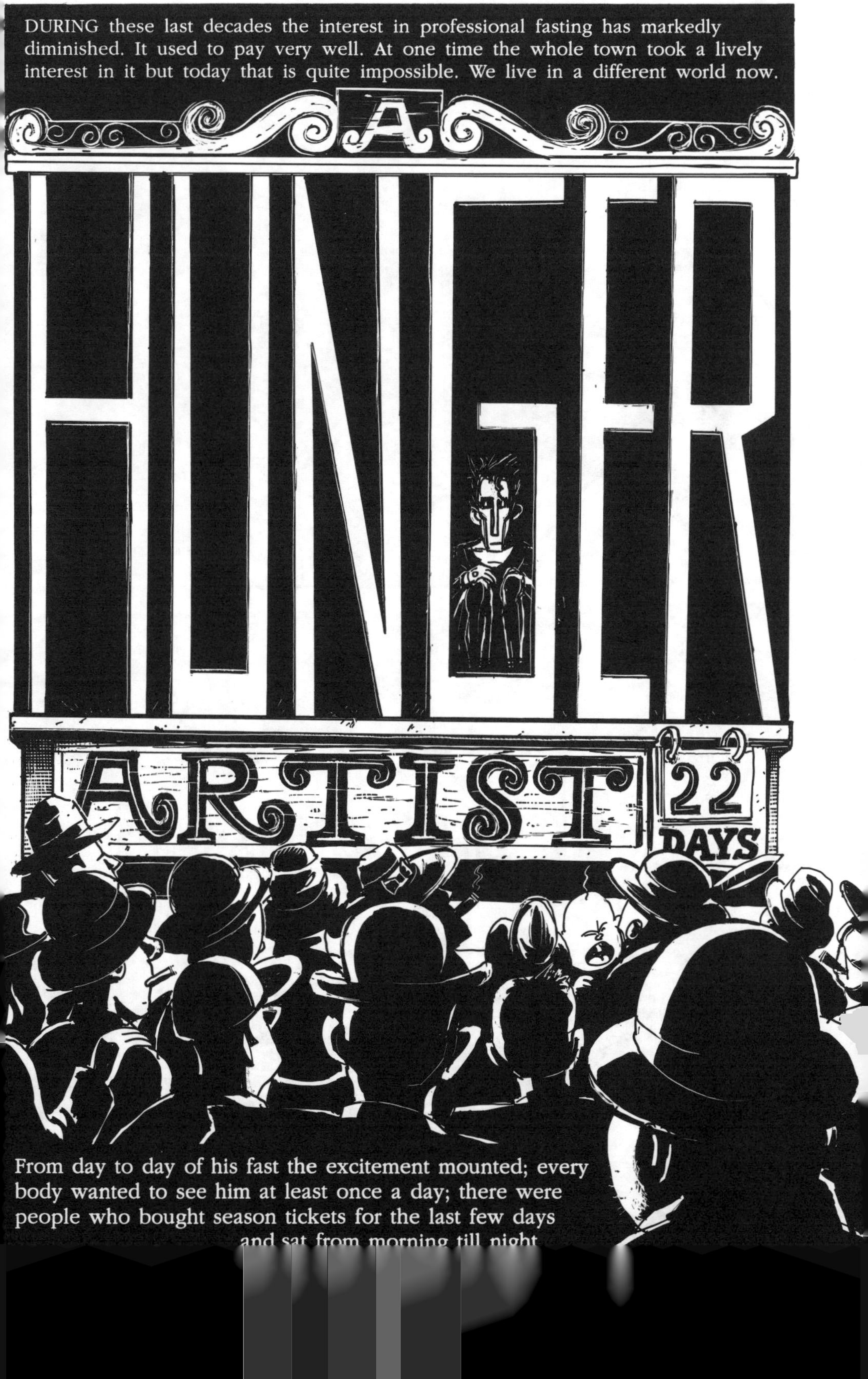
DURING these last decades the interest in professional fasting has markedly diminished. It used to pay very well. At one time the whole town took a lively interest in it but today that is quite impossible. We live in a different world now.
A
HUNGER
ARTIST
22
DAYS
From day to day of his fast the excitement mounted; every body wanted to see him at least once a day; there were people who bought season tickets for the last few days
and sat from morning till night

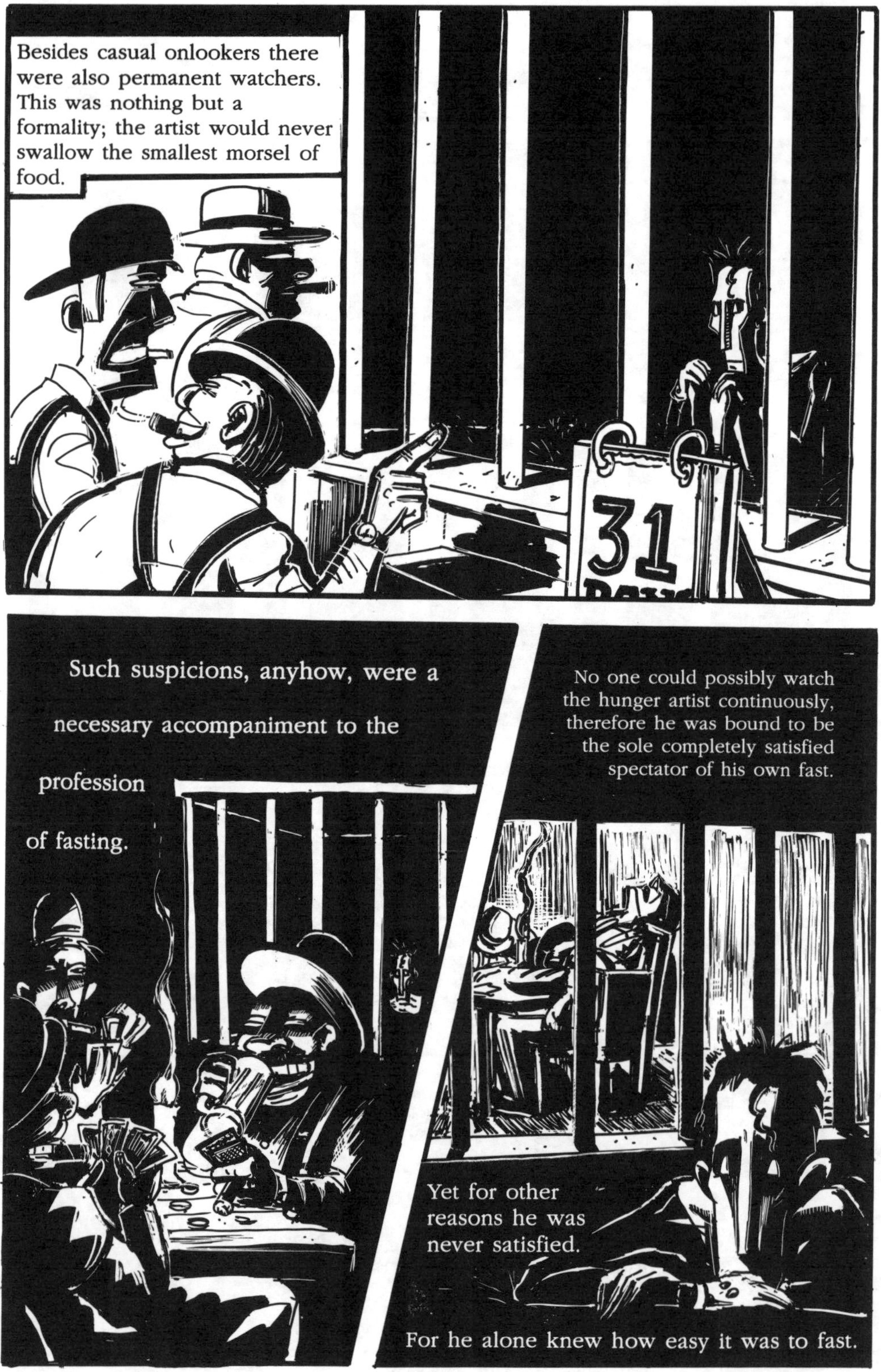
Besides casual onlookers there were also permanent watchers. This was nothing but a formality; the artist would never swallow the smallest morsel of food.
31
Such suspicions, anyhow, were a necessary accompaniment to the profession of fasting.
No one could possibly watch the hunger artist continuously, therefore he was bound to be the sole completely satisfied spectator of his own fast.
Yet for other reasons he was never satisfied.
For he alone knew how easy it was to fast.

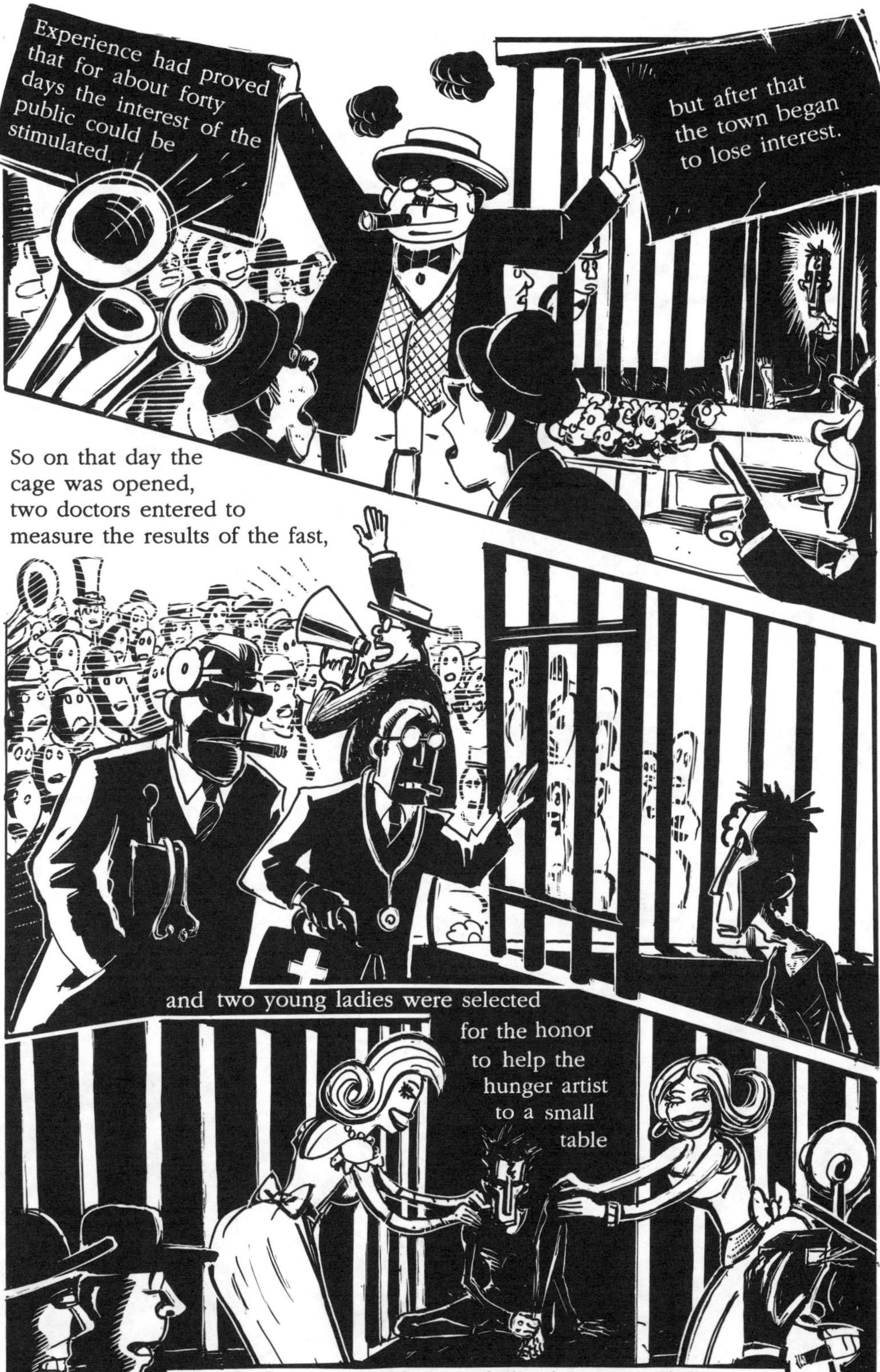
Experience had proved that for about forty days the interest of the public could be stimulated,
but after that the town began to lose interest.
So on that day the cage was opened, two doctors entered to measure the results of the fast,
and two young ladies were selected
for the honor to help the hunger artist to a small table
on which was spread a carefully chosen invalid repast.

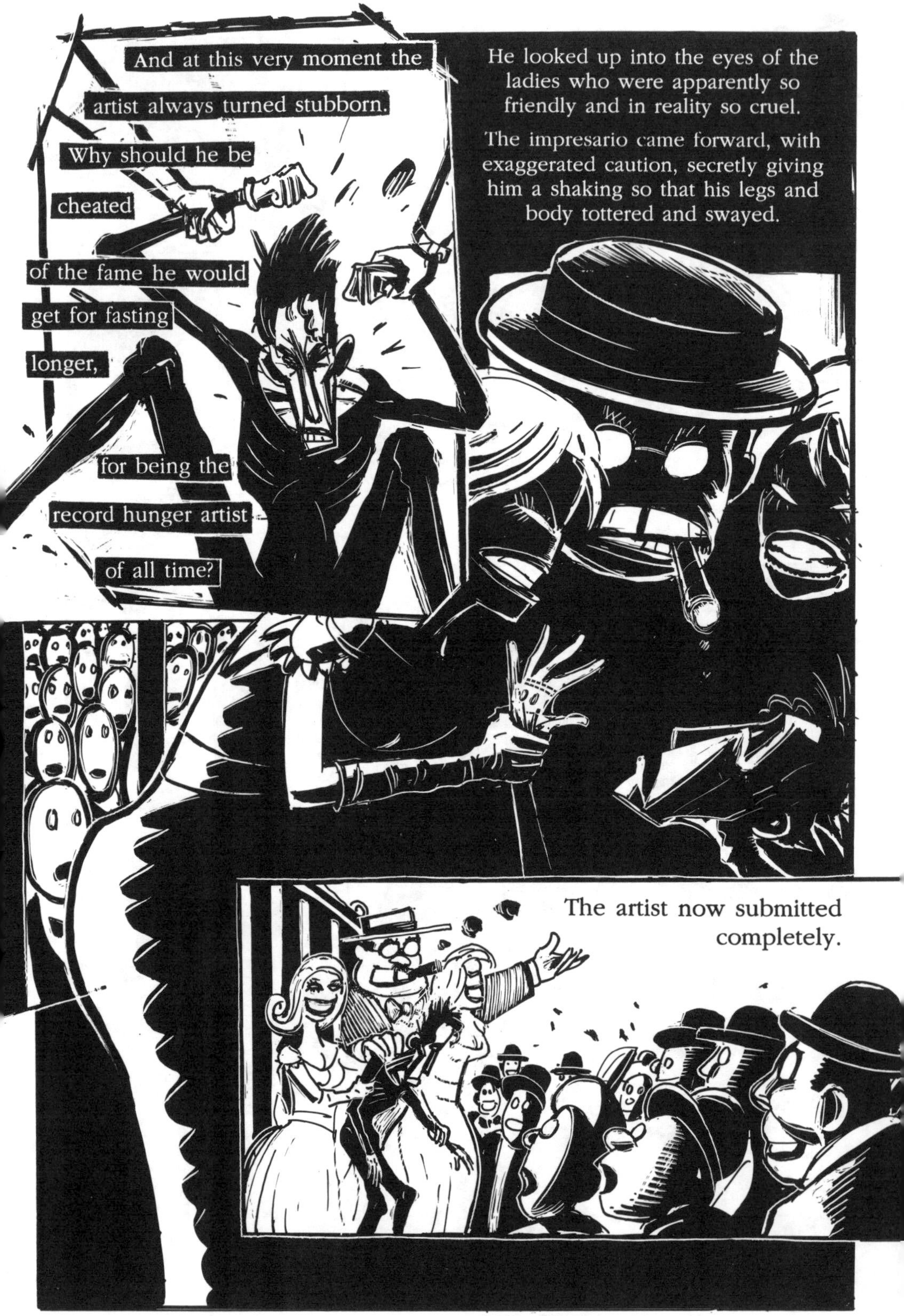

And at this very moment the
artist always turned stubborn.
Why should he be
cheated
of the fame he would
get for fasting
longer,
for being the
record hunger artist
of all time?
He looked up into the eyes of the ladies who were apparently so friendly and in reality so cruel.
The impresario came forward, with exaggerated caution, secretly giving him a shaking so that his legs and body tottered and swayed.
The artist now submitted completely.

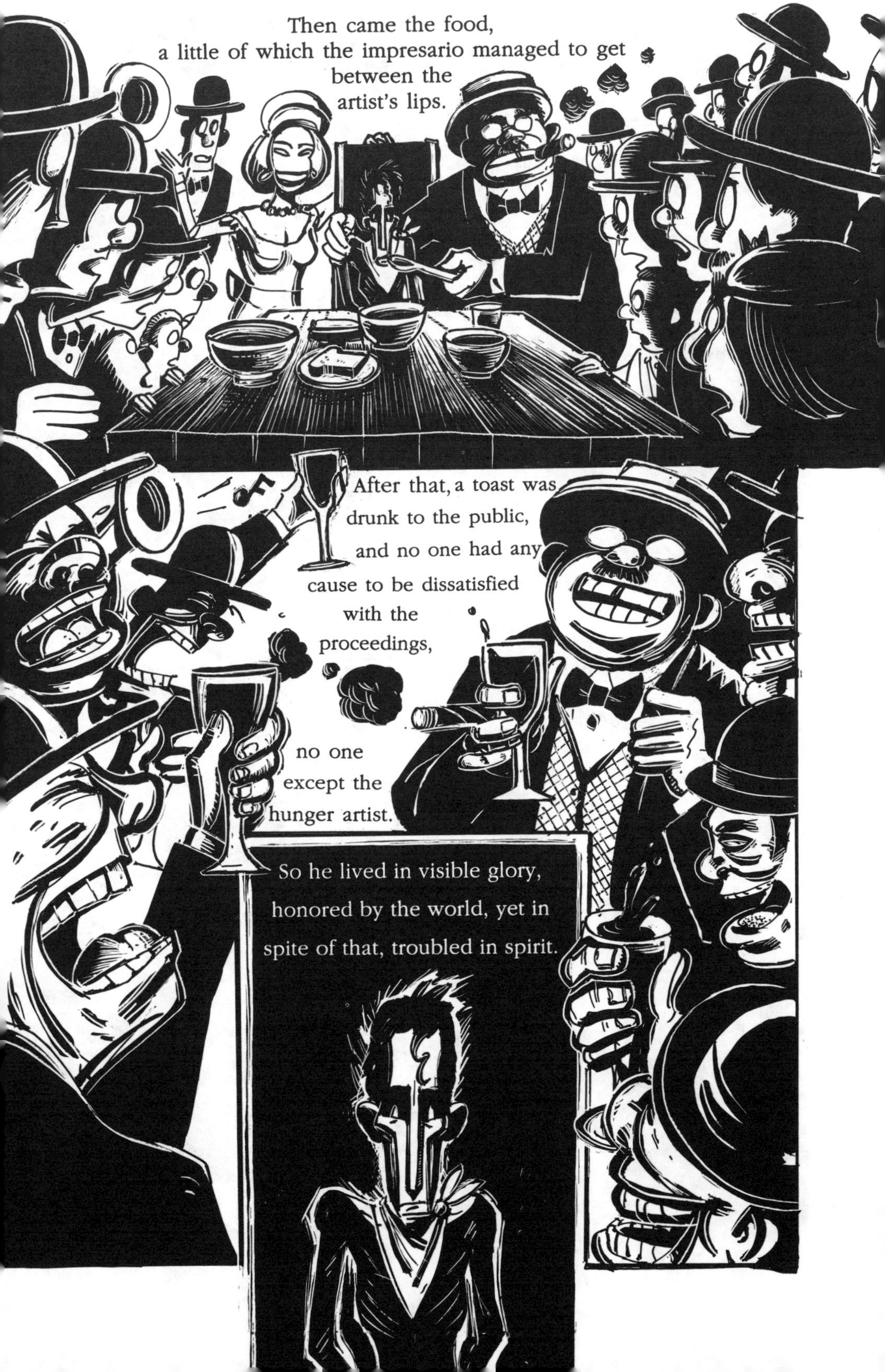
Then came the food, a little of which the impresario managed to get between the artist's lips.
After that, a toast was drunk to the public, and no one had any cause to be dissatisfied with the proceedings,
no one except the hunger artist.
So he lived in visible glory, honored by the world, yet in spite of that, troubled in spirit.

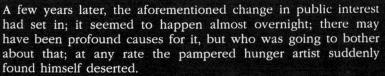

A few years later, the aforementioned change in public interest had set in; it seemed to happen almost overnight; there may have been profound causes for it, but who was going to bother about that; at any rate the pampered hunger artist suddenly found himself deserted.

So he took leave of the impresario,

and hired himself to a large circus;

WORLD'S-☆-GREAT
HUNGER ARTIST

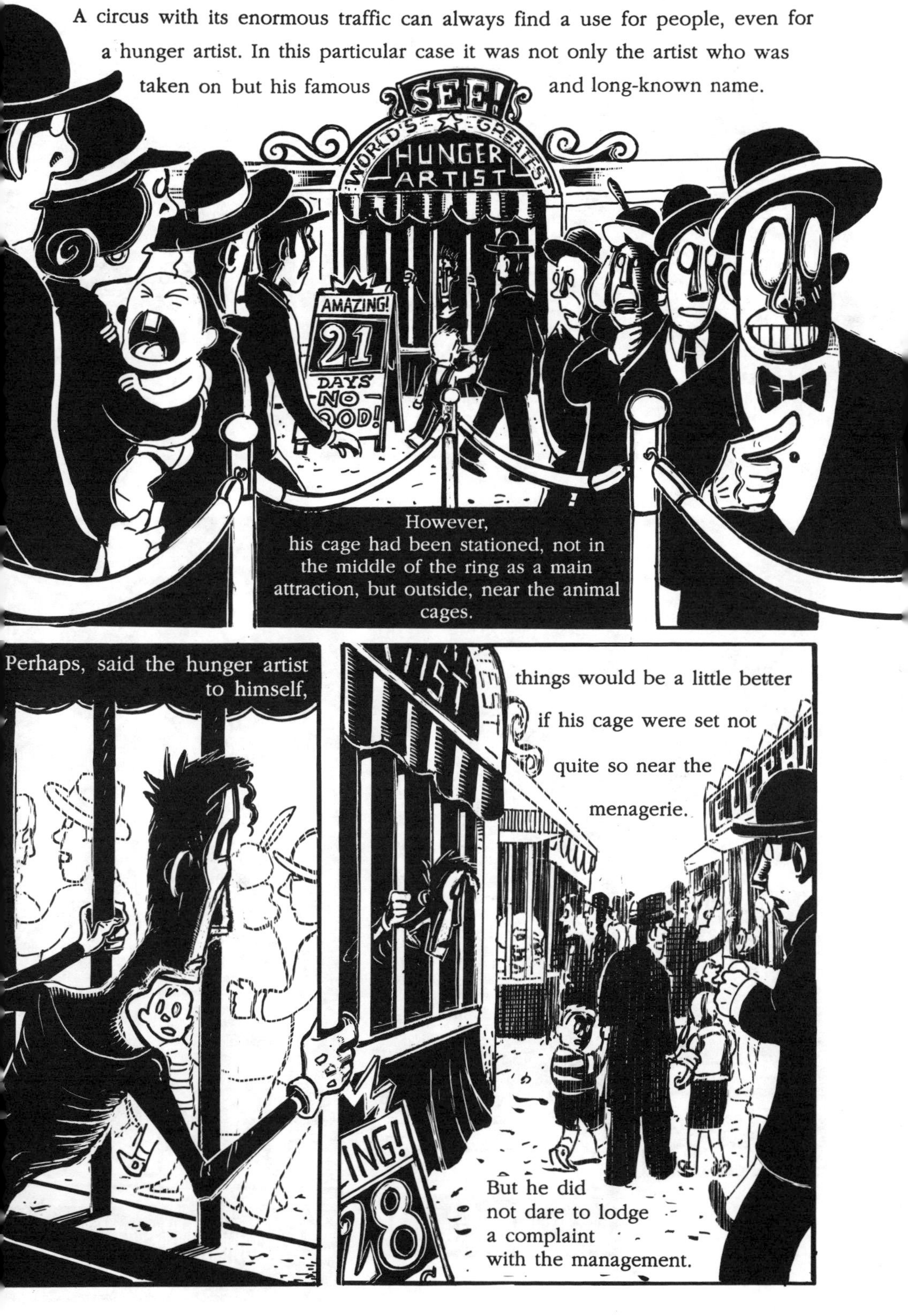
A circus with its enormous traffic can always find a use for people, even for a hunger artist. In this particular case it was not only the artist who was taken on but his famous
SEE!
WORLD'S ★ GREATEST
HUNGER ARTIST
and long-known name.
AMAZING!
21
DAYS
NO
However, his cage had been stationed, not in the middle of the ring as a main attraction, but outside, near the animal cages.
Perhaps, said the hunger artist to himself,
things would be a little better if his cage were set not quite so near the menagerie.
ING!
But he did not dare to lodge a complaint with the management.

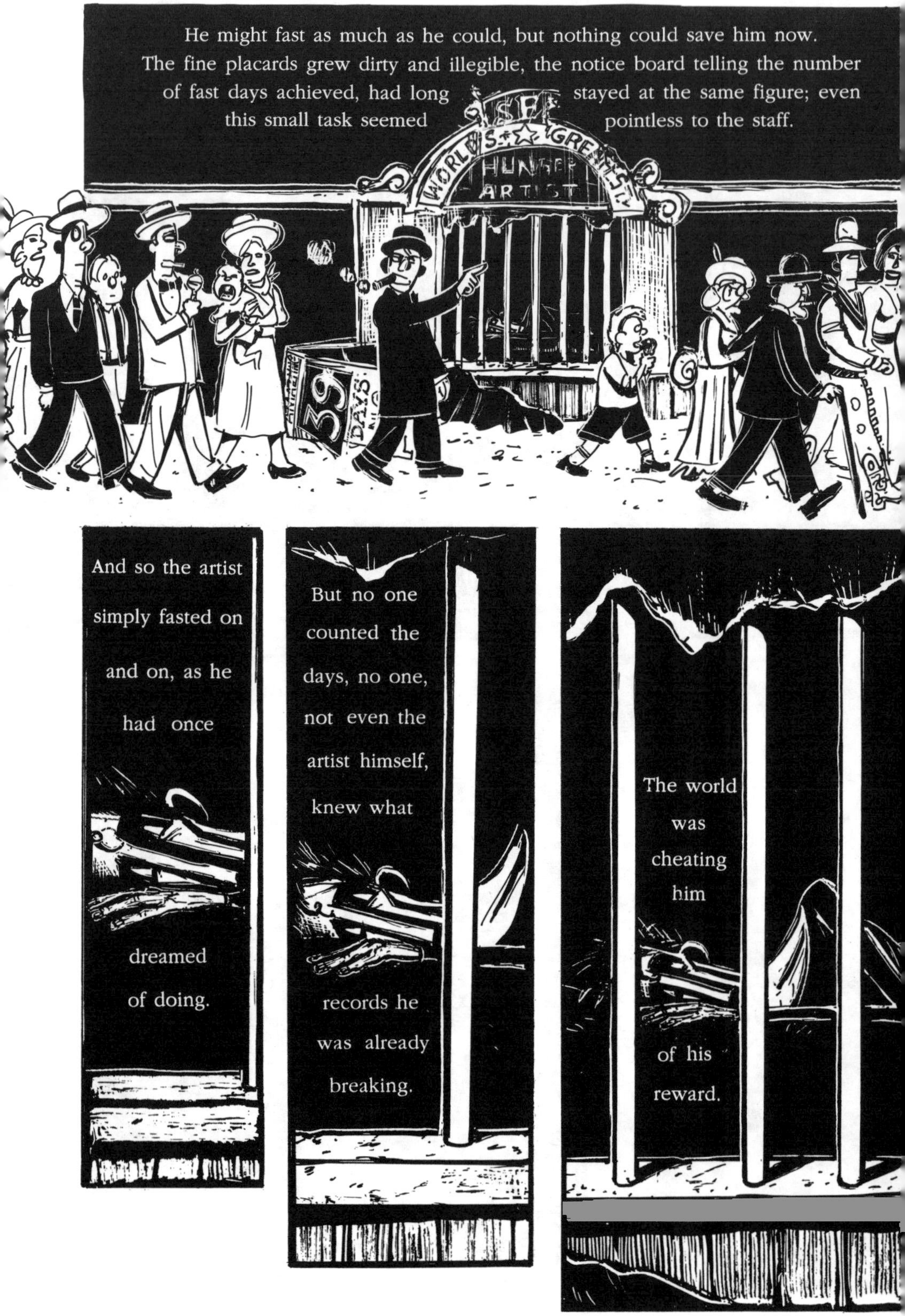
He might fast as much as he could, but nothing could save him now. The fine placards grew dirty and illegible, the notice board telling the number of fast days achieved, had long stayed at the same figure; even this small task seemed pointless to the staff.
39
And so the artist simply fasted on and on, as he had once dreamed of doing.
But no one counted the days, no one, not even the artist himself, knew what records he was already breaking.
The world was cheating him of his reward.

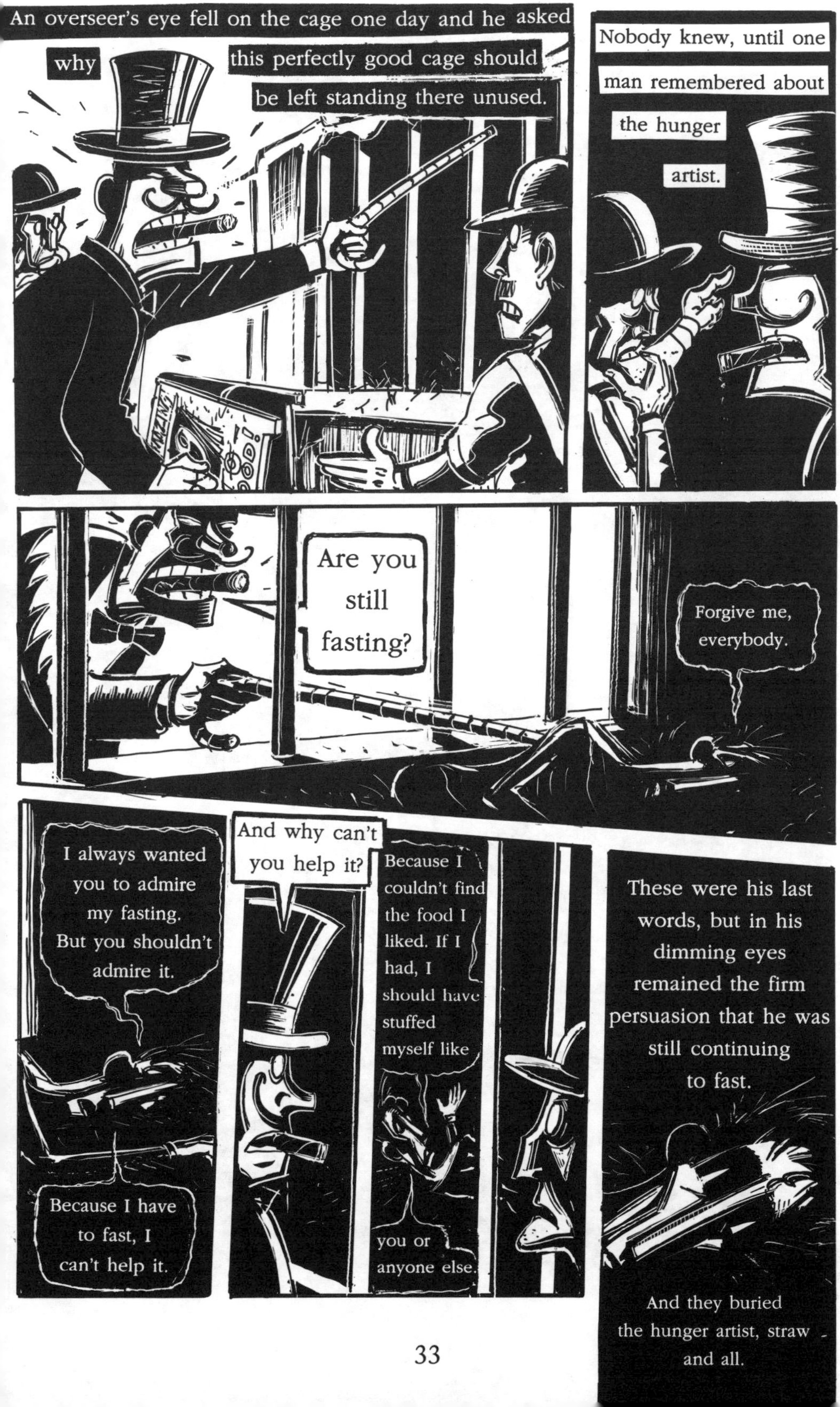
An overseer's eye fell on the cage one day and he asked
why
this perfectly good cage should
be left standing there unused.
Nobody knew, until one
man remembered about
the hunger
artist.
Are you still fasting?
Forgive me, everybody.
I always wanted you to admire my fasting. But you shouldn't admire it.
Because I have to fast, I can't help it.
And why can't you help it?
Because I couldn't find the food I liked. If I had, I should have stuffed myself like
you or anyone else.
These were his last words, but in his dimming eyes remained the firm persuasion that he was still continuing to fast.
And they buried the hunger artist, straw and all.

Into the cage they put a young panther.

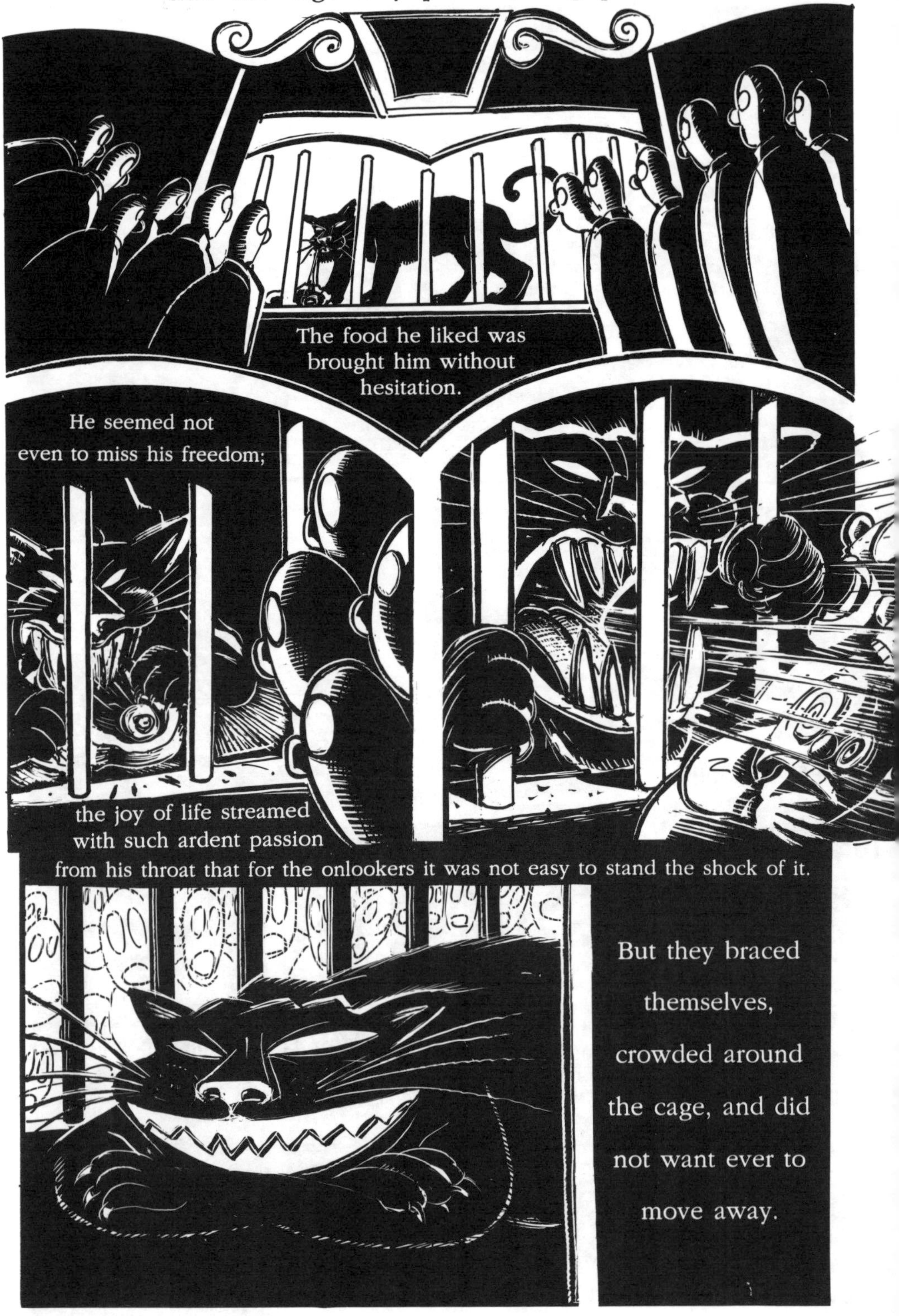

The food he liked was brought him without hesitation.
He seemed not even to miss his freedom;
the joy of life streamed with such ardent passion
from his throat that for the onlookers it was not easy to stand the shock of it.
But they braced themselves, crowded around the cage, and did not want ever to move away.

A Fratricide

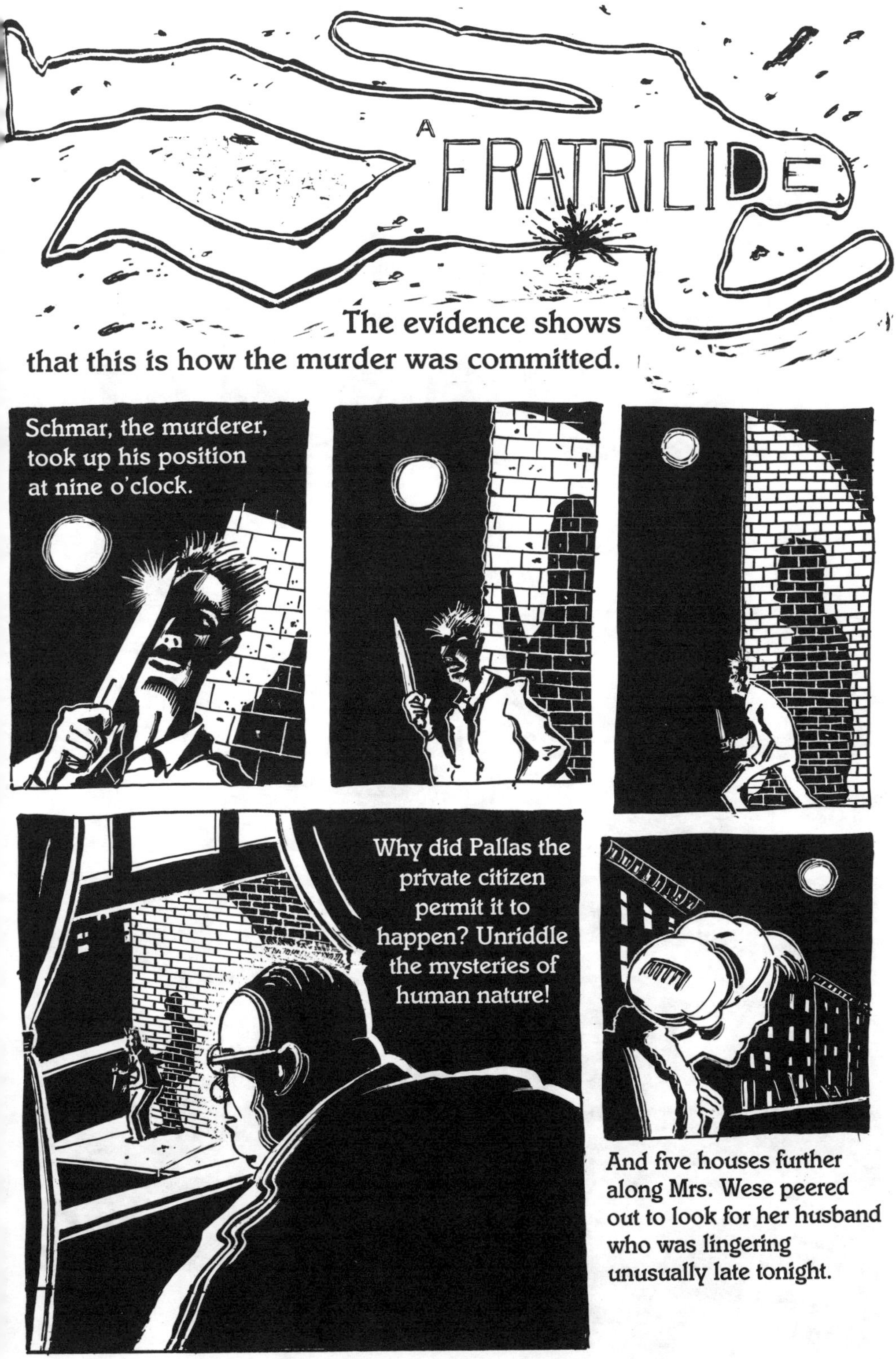
A FRATRICIDE
The evidence shows that this is how the murder was committed.
Schmar, the murderer, took up his position at nine o'clock.
Why did Pallas the private citizen permit it to happen? Unriddle the mysteries of human nature!
And five houses further along Mrs. Wese peered out to look for her husband who was lingering unusually late tonight.

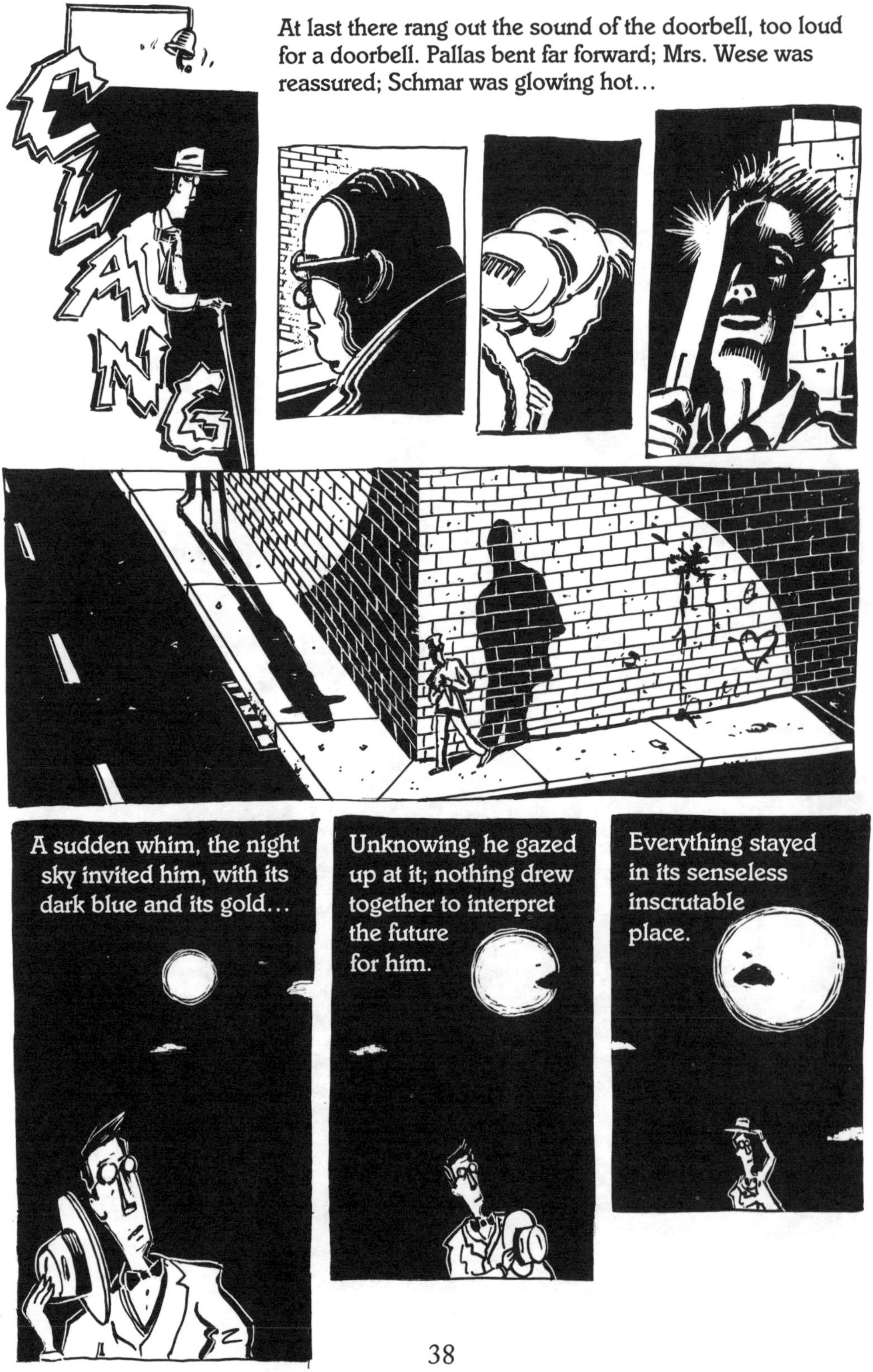
CLANG
At last there rang out the sound of the doorbell, too loud for a doorbell. Pallas bent far forward; Mrs. Wese was reassured; Schmar was glowing hot…
A sudden whim, the night sky invited him, with its dark blue and its gold…
Unknowing, he gazed up at it; nothing drew together to interpret the future for him.
Everything stayed in its senseless inscrutable place.

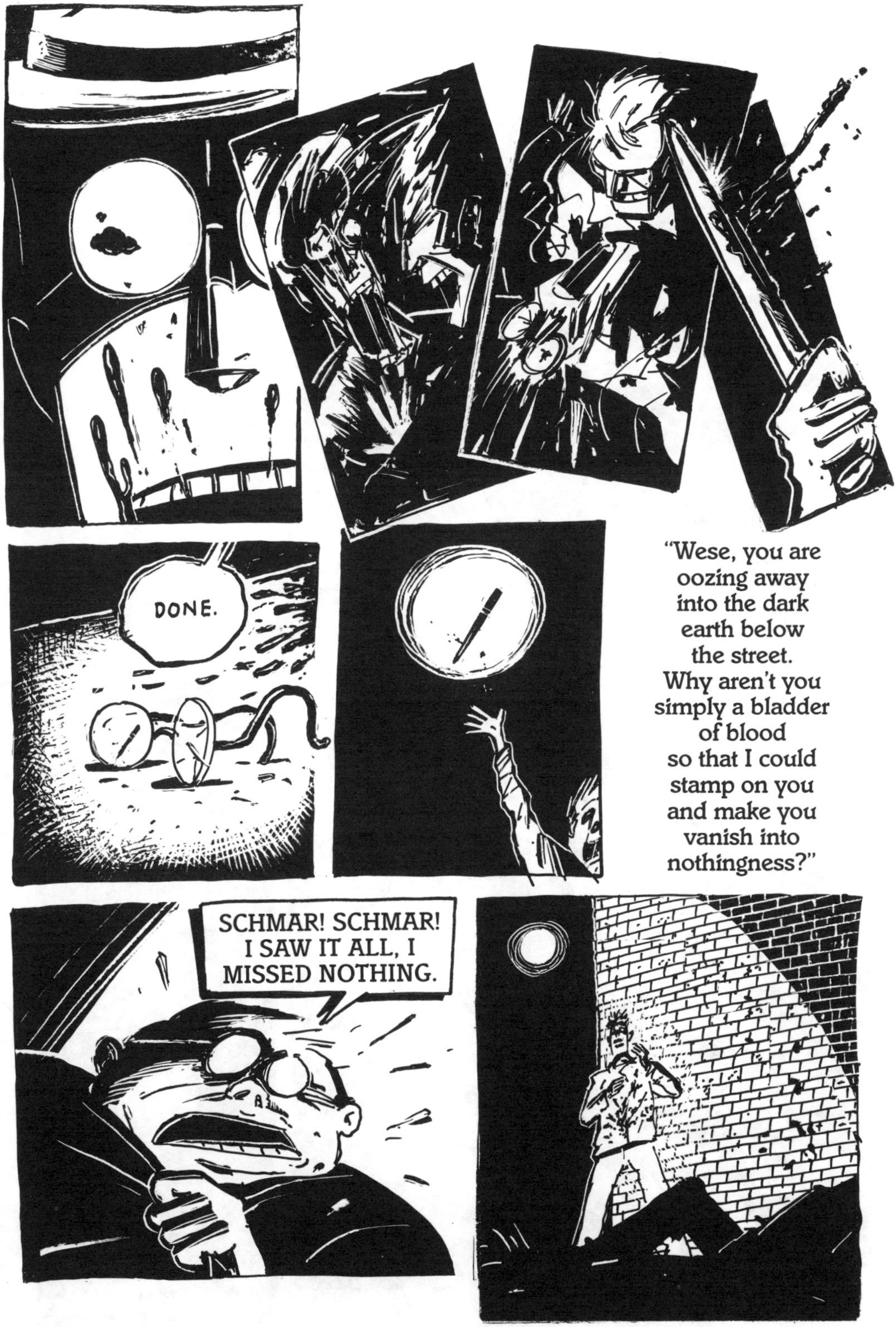
DONE.
"Wese, you are oozing away into the dark earth below the street. Why aren't you simply a bladder of blood so that I could stamp on you and make you vanish into nothingness?"
SCHMAR! SCHMAR! I SAW IT ALL, I MISSED NOTHING.

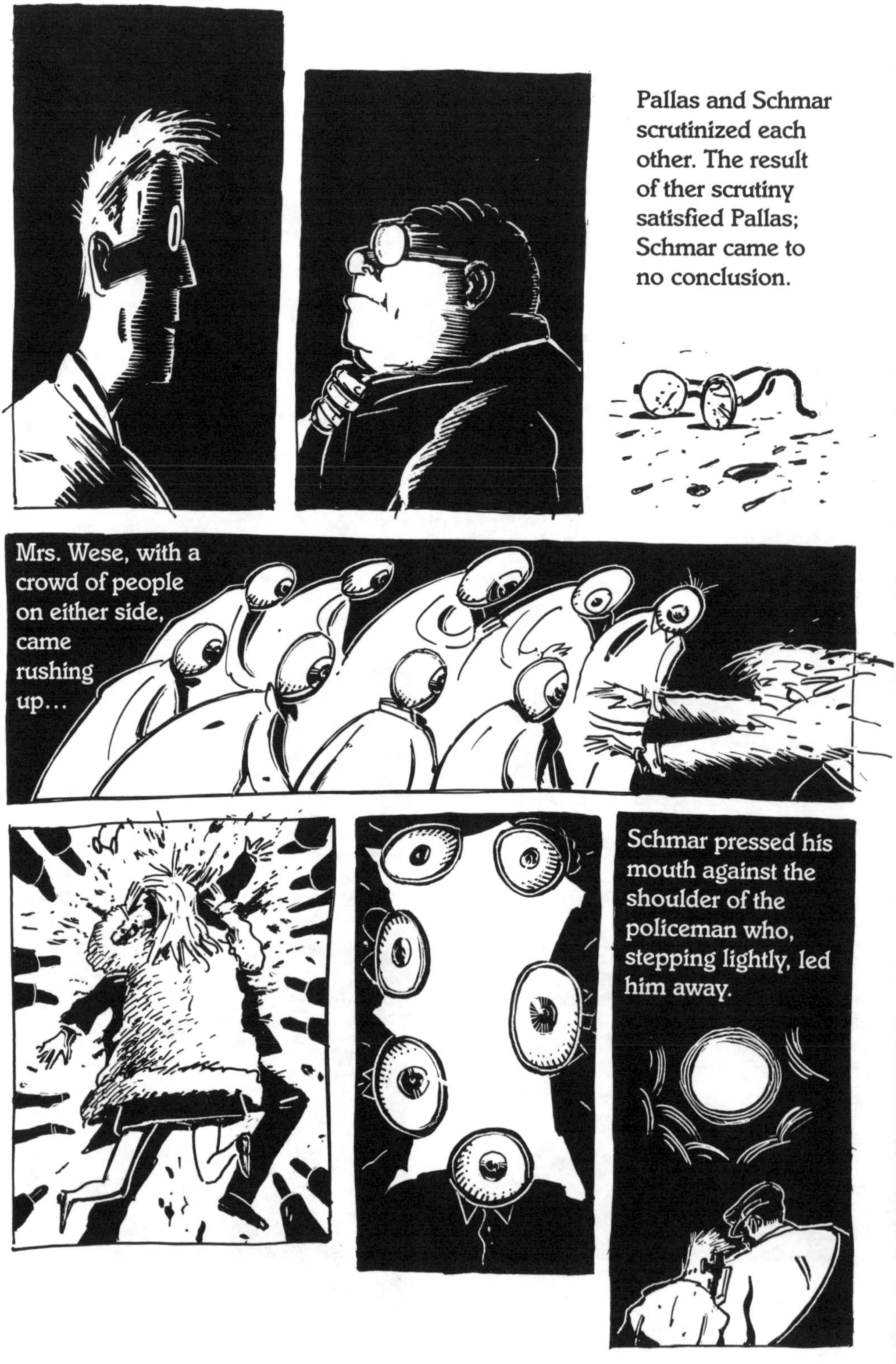
Pallas and Schmar scrutinized each other. The result of ther scrutiny satisfied Pallas; Schmar came to no conclusion.
Mrs. Wese, with a crowd of people on either side, came rushing up...
Schmar pressed his mouth against the shoulder of the policeman who, stepping lightly, led him away.

The Helmsman

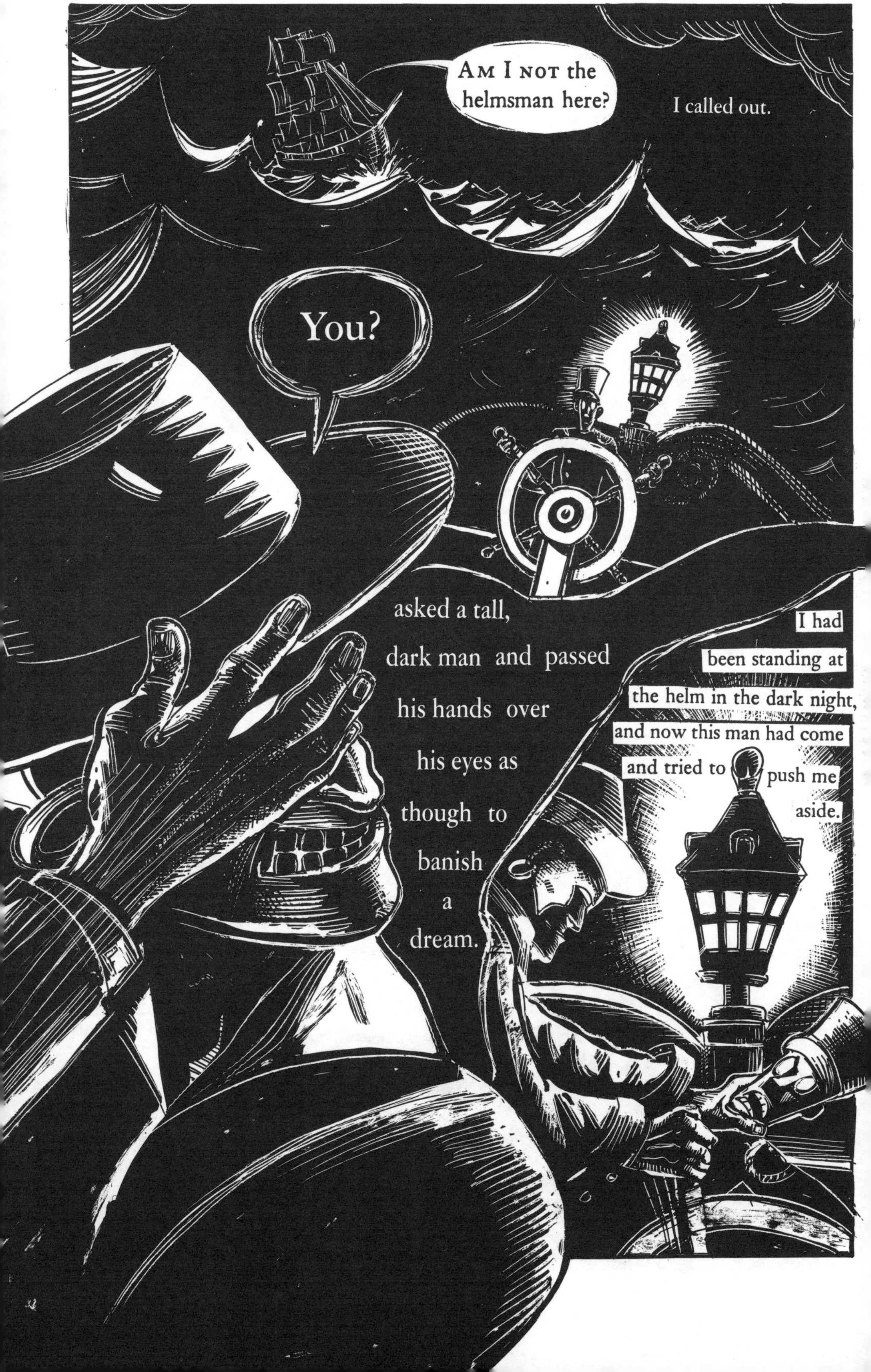

Am I not the helmsman here?
I called out.
You?
asked a tall, dark man and passed his hands over his eyes as though to banish a dream.
I had been standing at the helm in the dark night, and now this man had come and tried to push me aside.

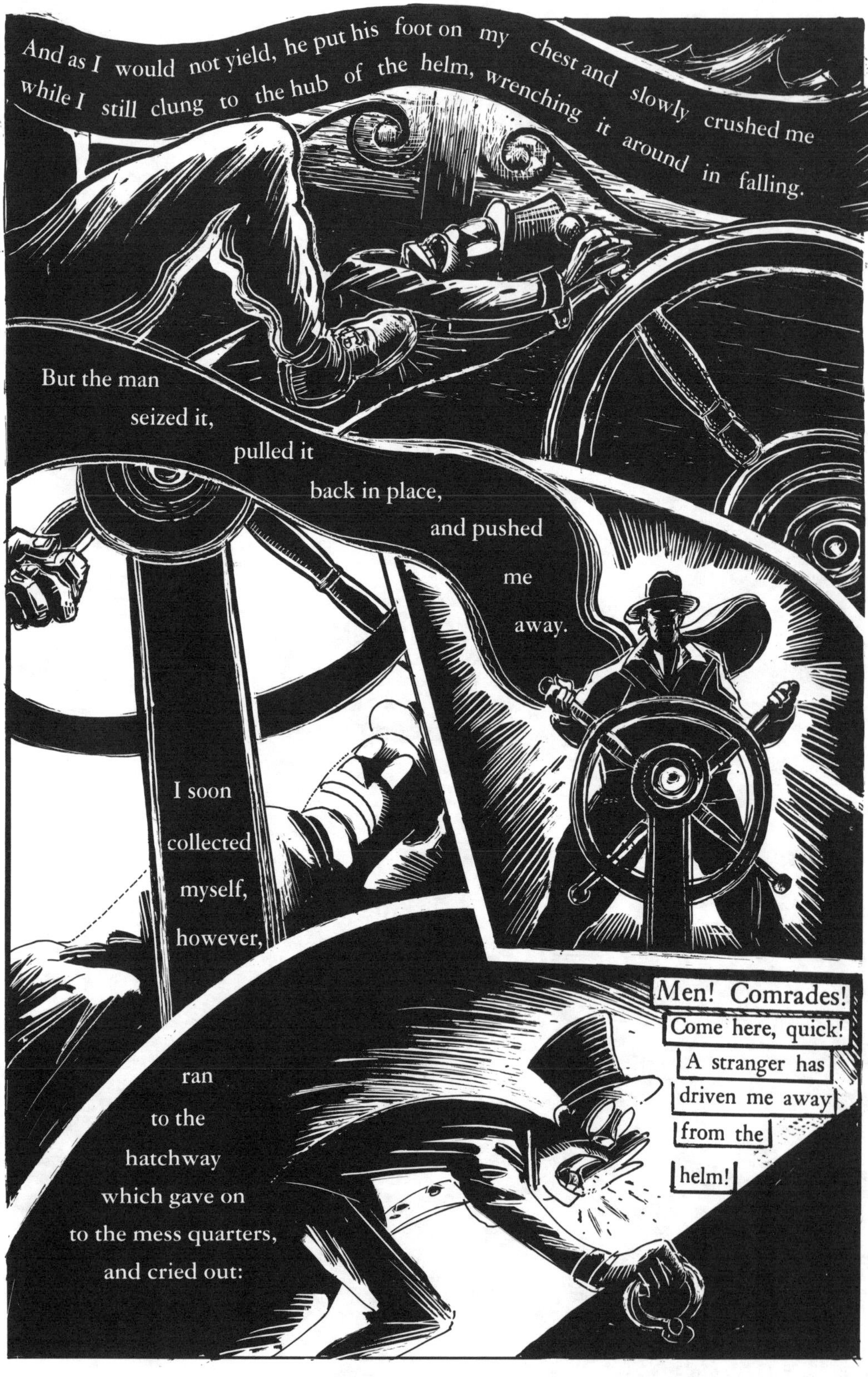

And as I would not yield, he put his foot on my chest and slowly crushed me while I still clung to the hub of the helm, wrenching it around in falling.
But the man seized it, pulled it back in place, and pushed me away.
I soon collected myself, however,
ran to the hatchway which gave on to the mess quarters, and cried out:
Men! Comrades!
Come here, quick!
A stranger has driven me away from the helm!

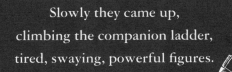

Slowly they came up,
climbing the companion ladder,
tired, swaying, powerful figures.

Am I
the
helmsman?

They nodded,

but they had

eyes only

for the stranger,

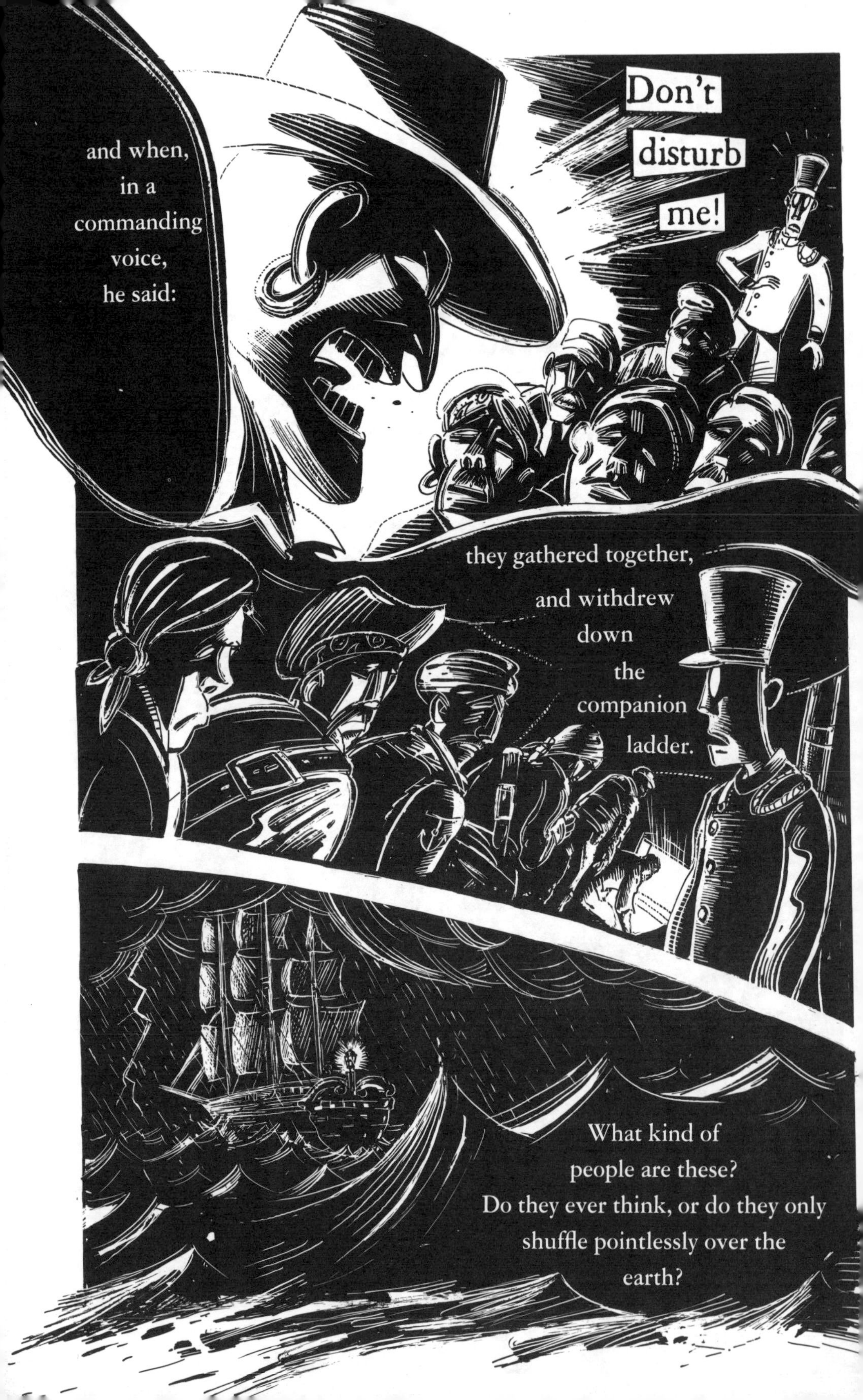
and when, in a commanding voice, he said:
Don't disturb me!
they gathered together, and withdrew down the companion ladder.
What kind of people are these? Do they ever think, or do they only shuffle pointlessly over the earth?

The Trees

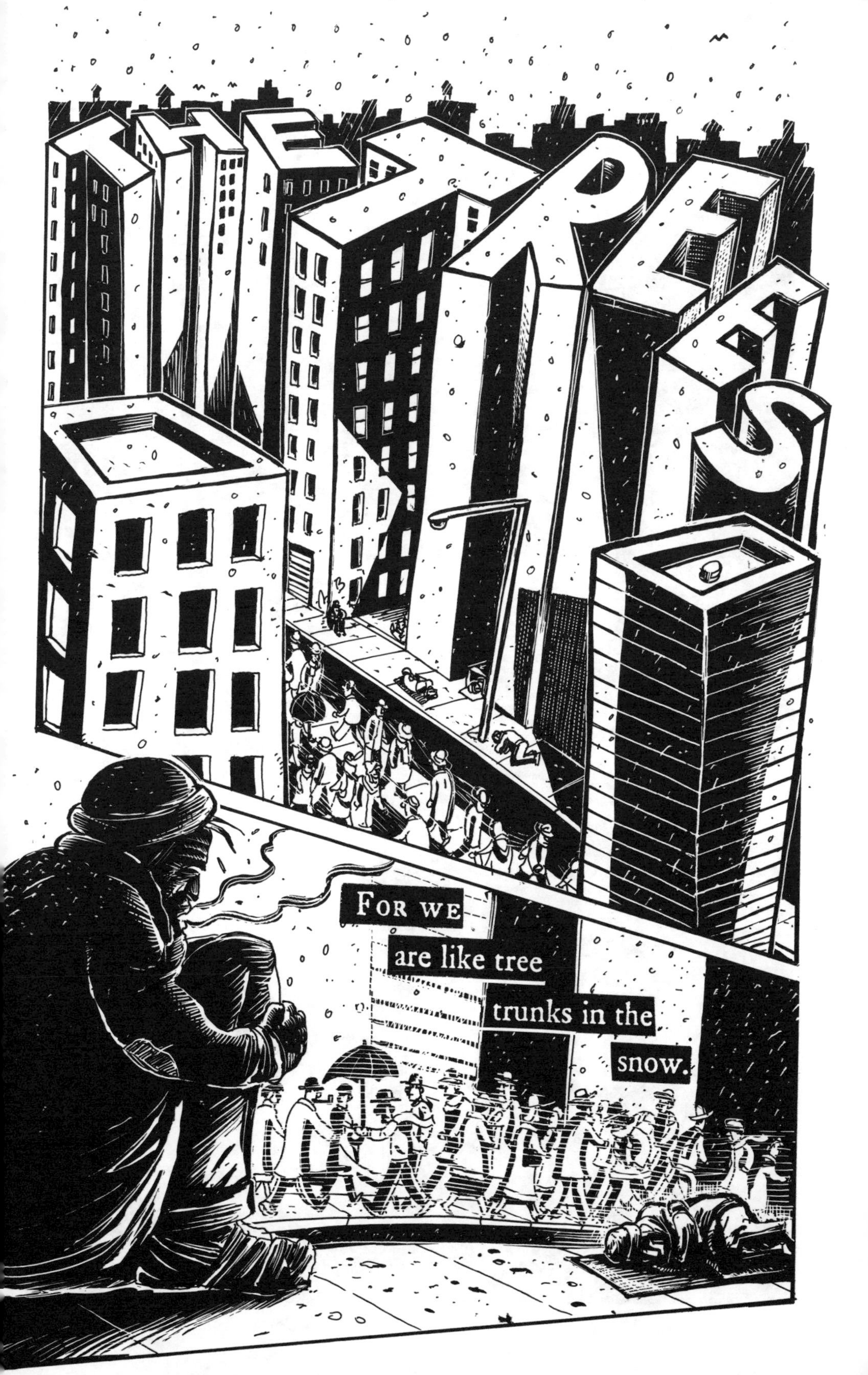
THE TREES
For we
are like tree
trunks in the
snow.

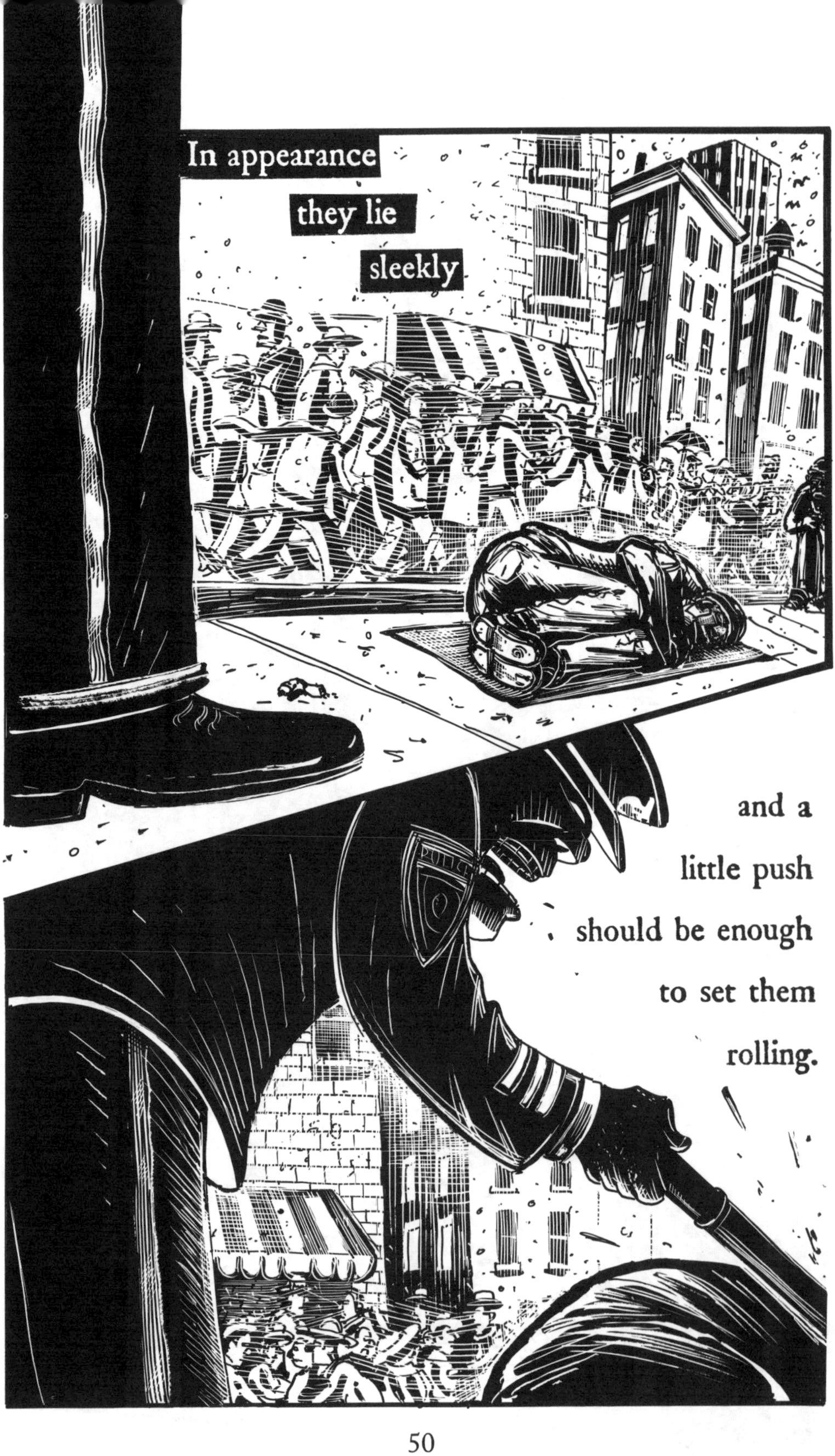
In appearance
they lie
sleekly
and a
little push
should be enough
to set them
rolling.

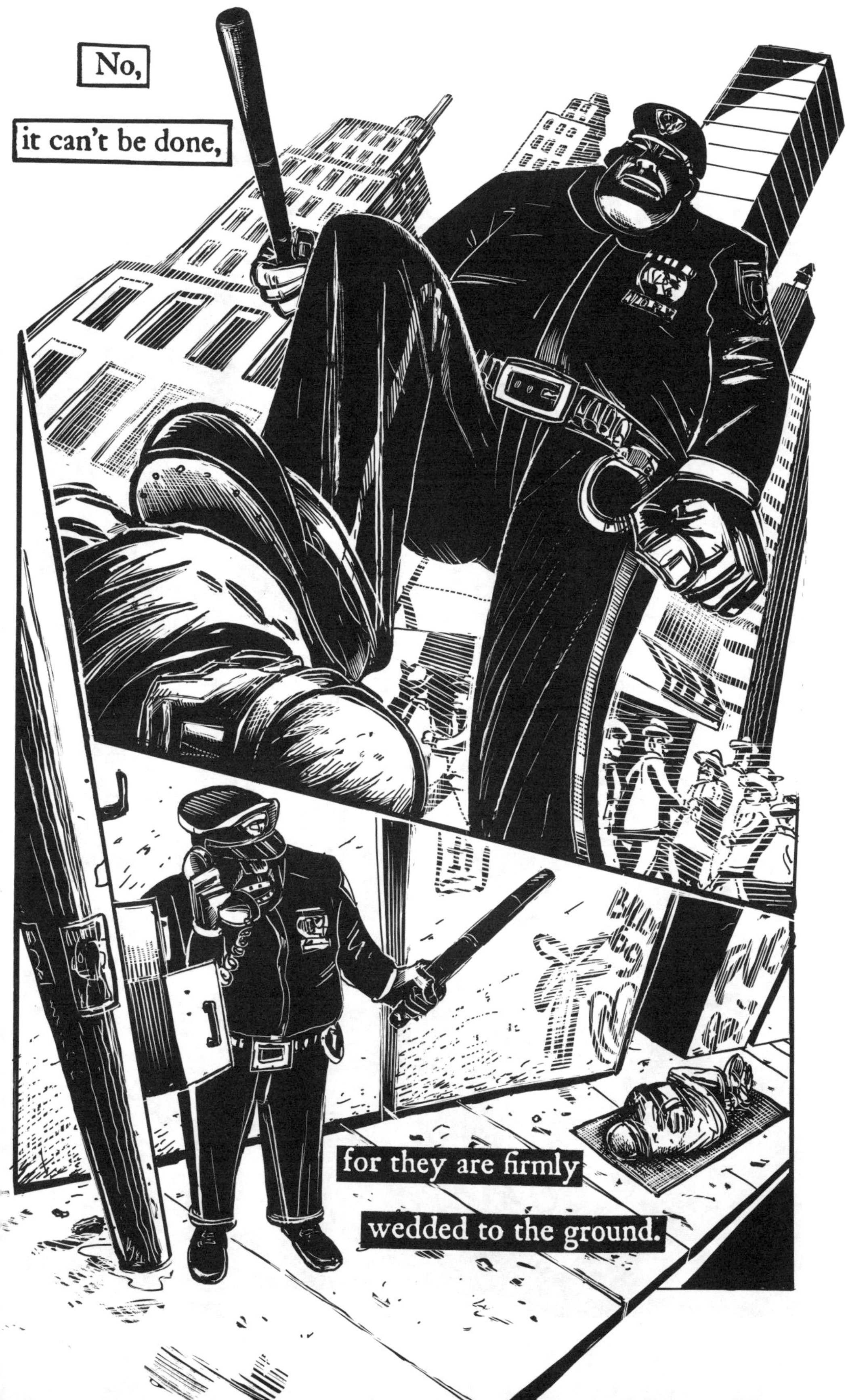
No,
it can't be done,
for they are firmly
wedded to the ground.

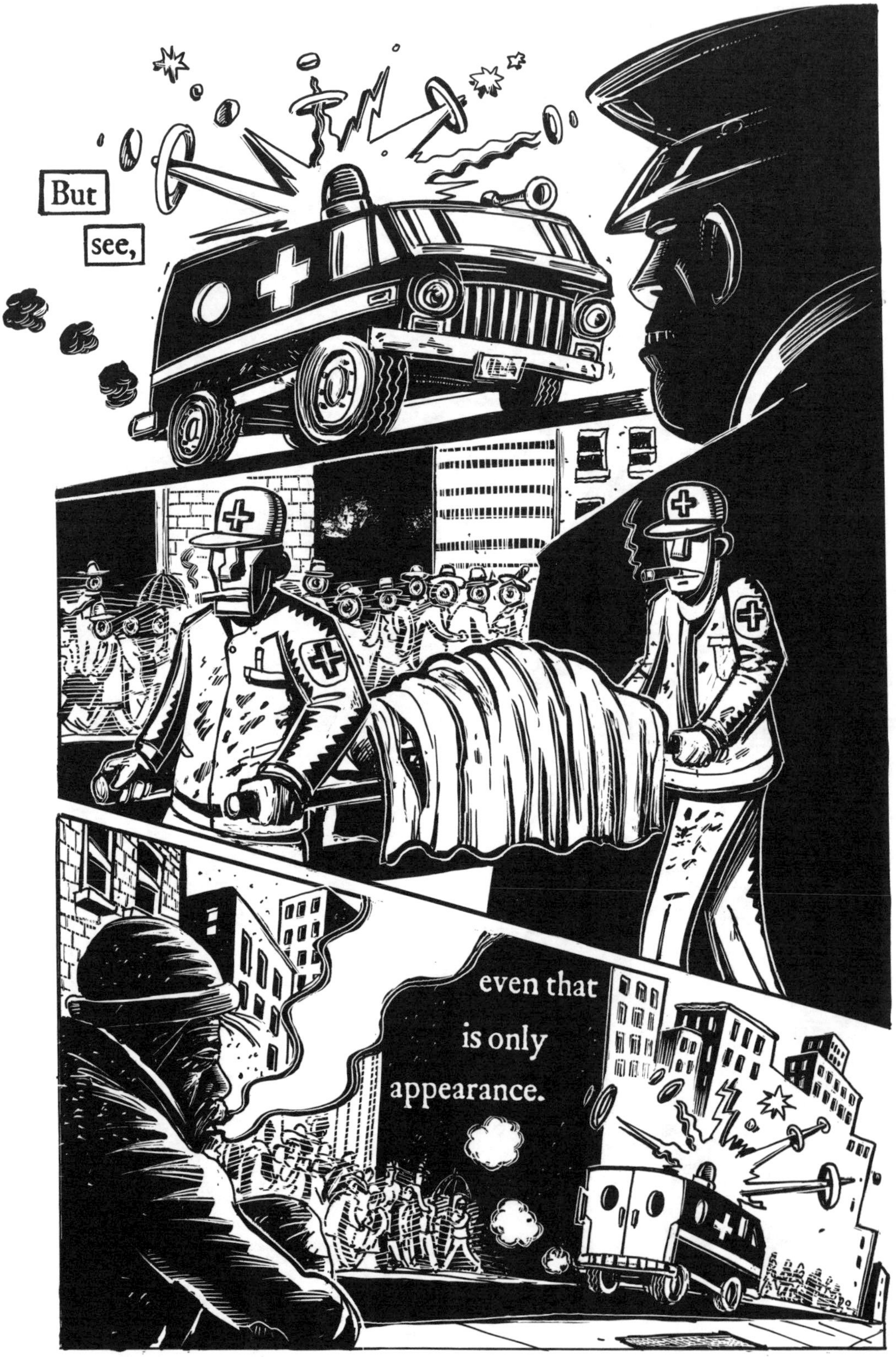
But
see,
even that
is only
appearance.

The Top

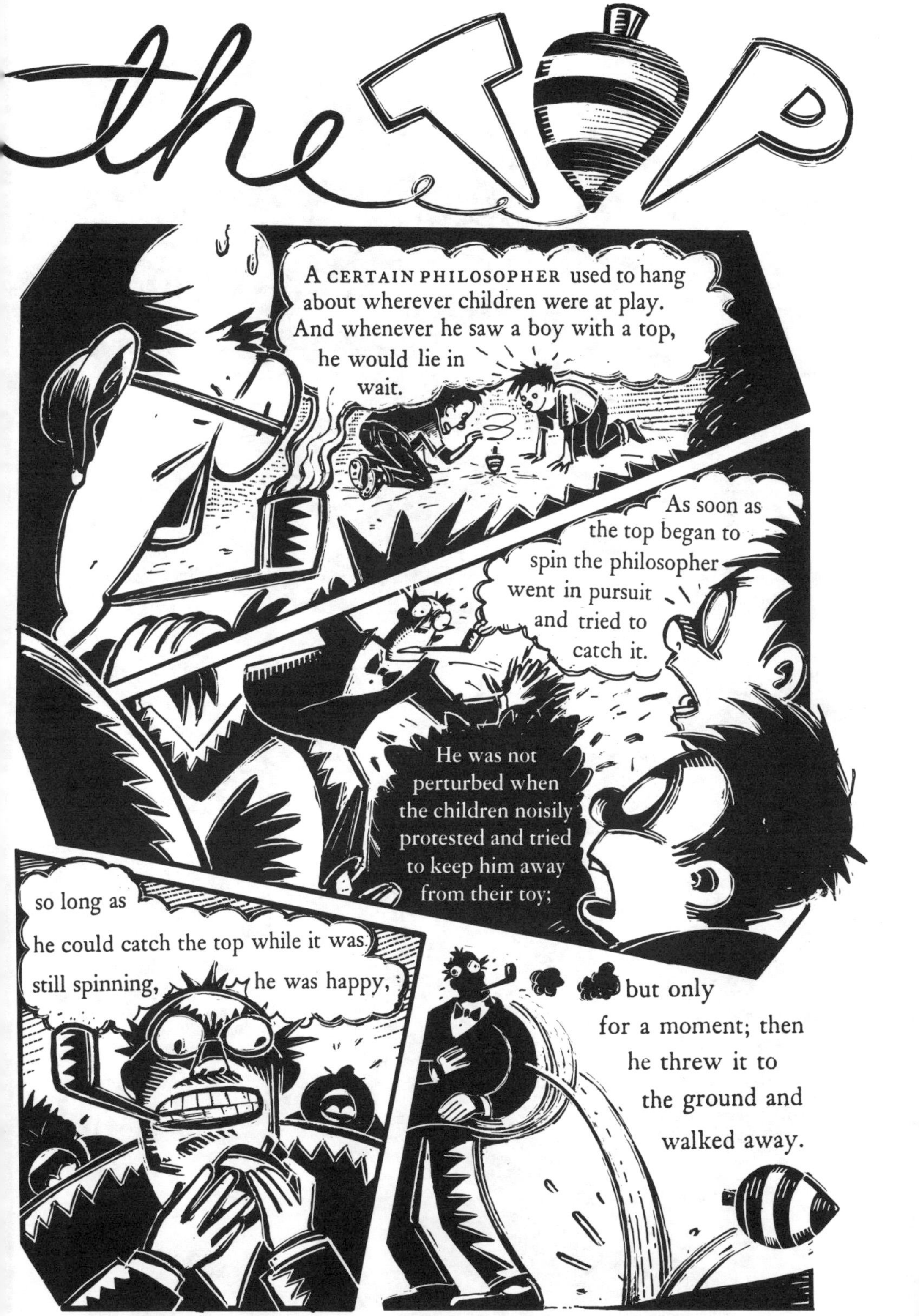
the TOP
A CERTAIN PHILOSOPHER used to hang about wherever children were at play. And whenever he saw a boy with a top, he would lie in wait.
As soon as the top began to spin the philosopher went in pursuit and tried to catch it.
He was not perturbed when the children noisily protested and tried to keep him away from their toy;
so long as he could catch the top while it was still spinning, he was happy,
but only for a moment; then he threw it to the ground and walked away.

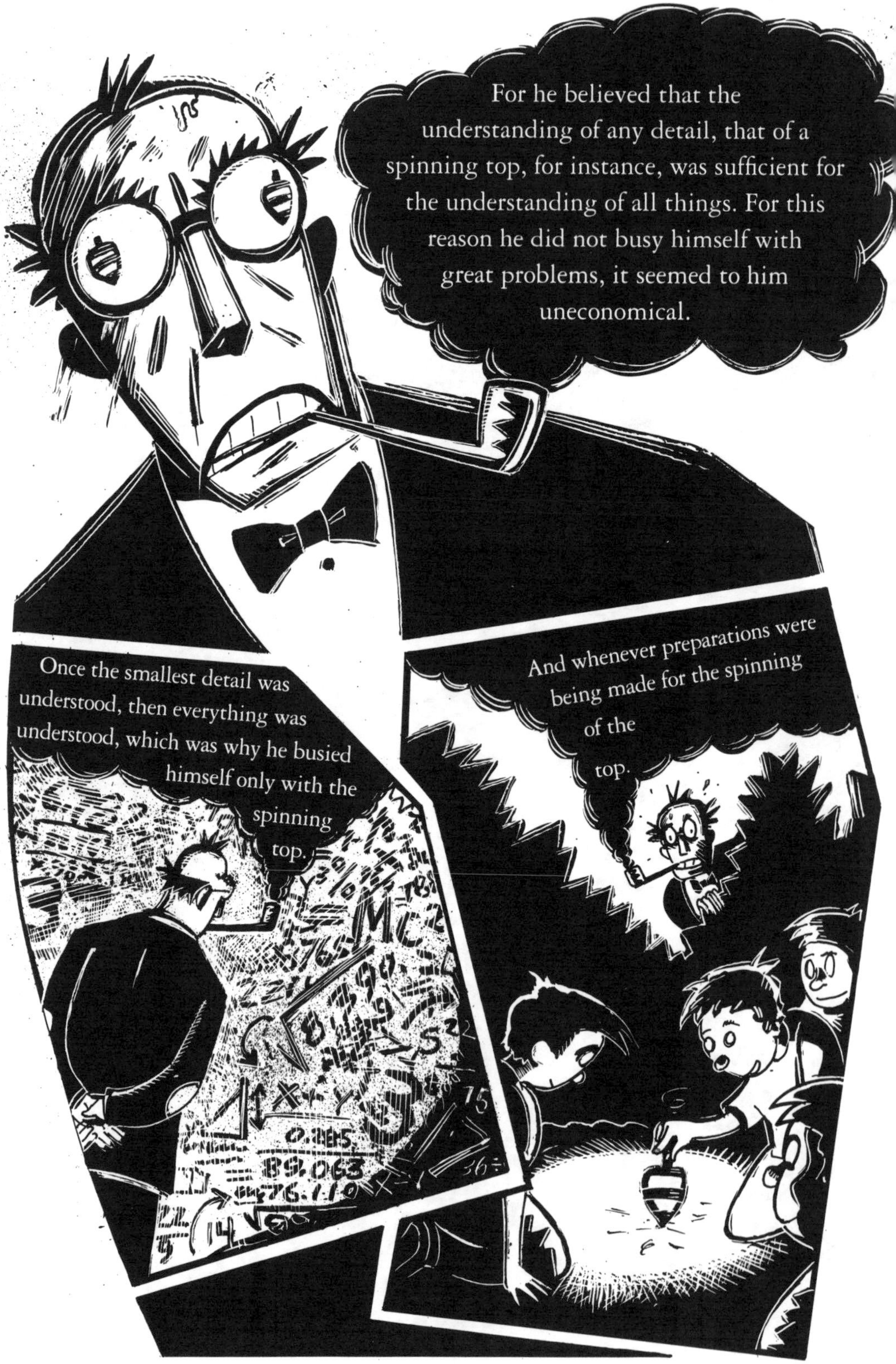
For he believed that the understanding of any detail, that of a spinning top, for instance, was sufficient for the understanding of all things. For this reason he did not busy himself with great problems, it seemed to him uneconomical.
Once the smallest detail was understood, then everything was understood, which was why he busied himself only with the spinning top.
And whenever preparations were being made for the spinning of the top.

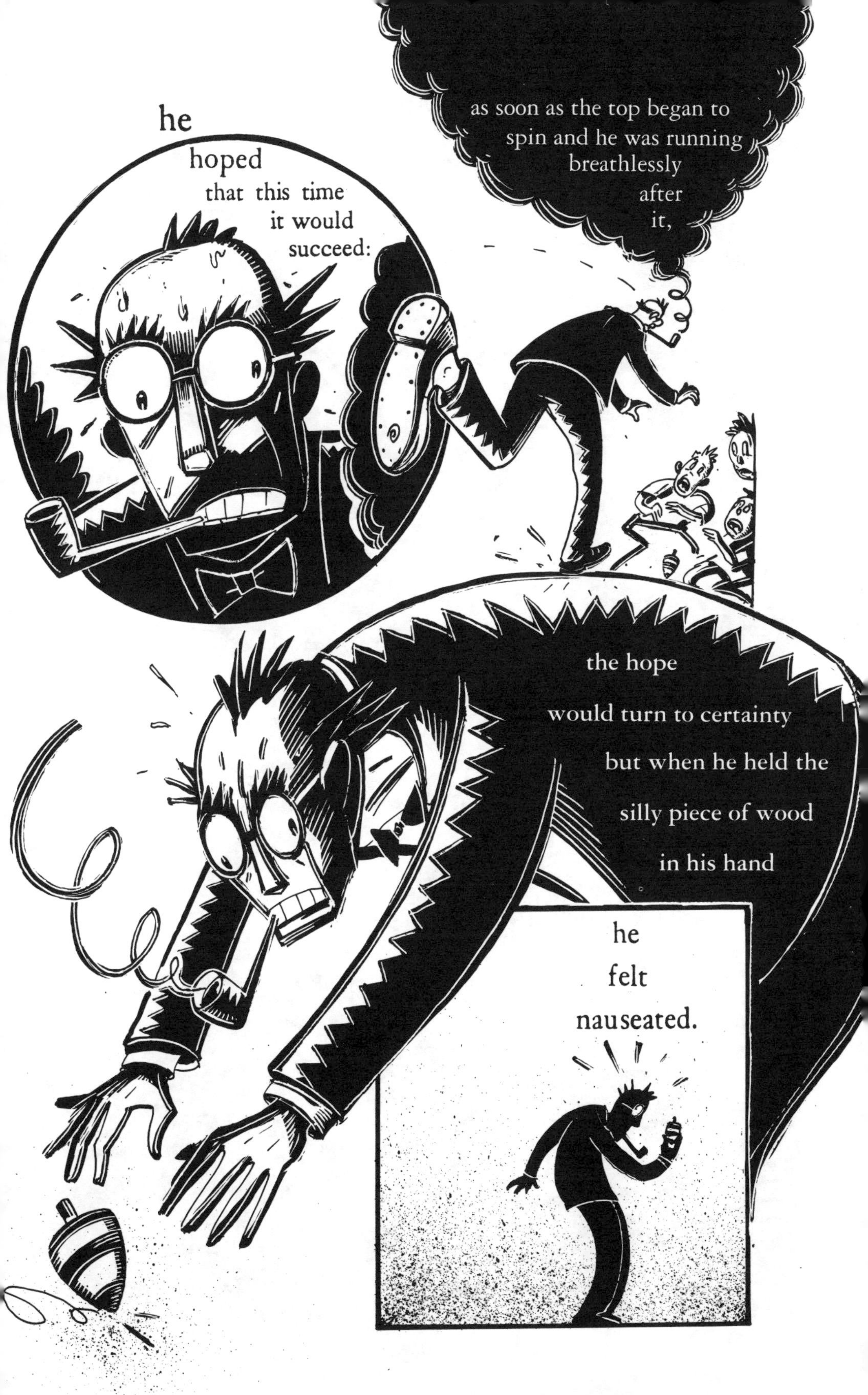
he hoped that this time it would succeed:
as soon as the top began to spin and he was running breathlessly after it,
the hope would turn to certainty
but when he held the silly piece of wood in his hand
he felt nauseated.

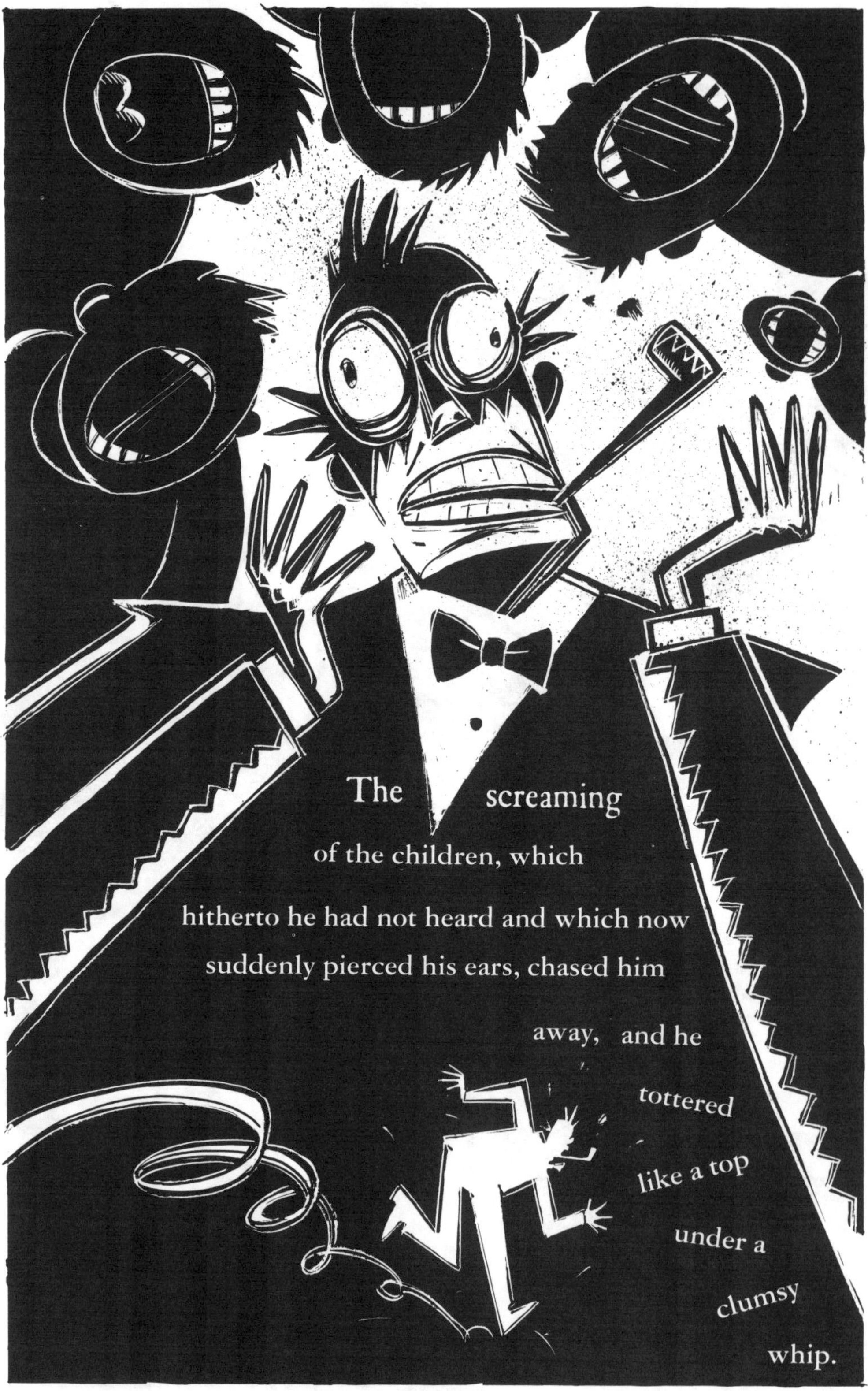
The screaming
of the children, which
hitherto he had not heard and which now
suddenly pierced his ears, chased him
away, and he
tottered
like a top
under a
clumsy
whip.

The Vulture

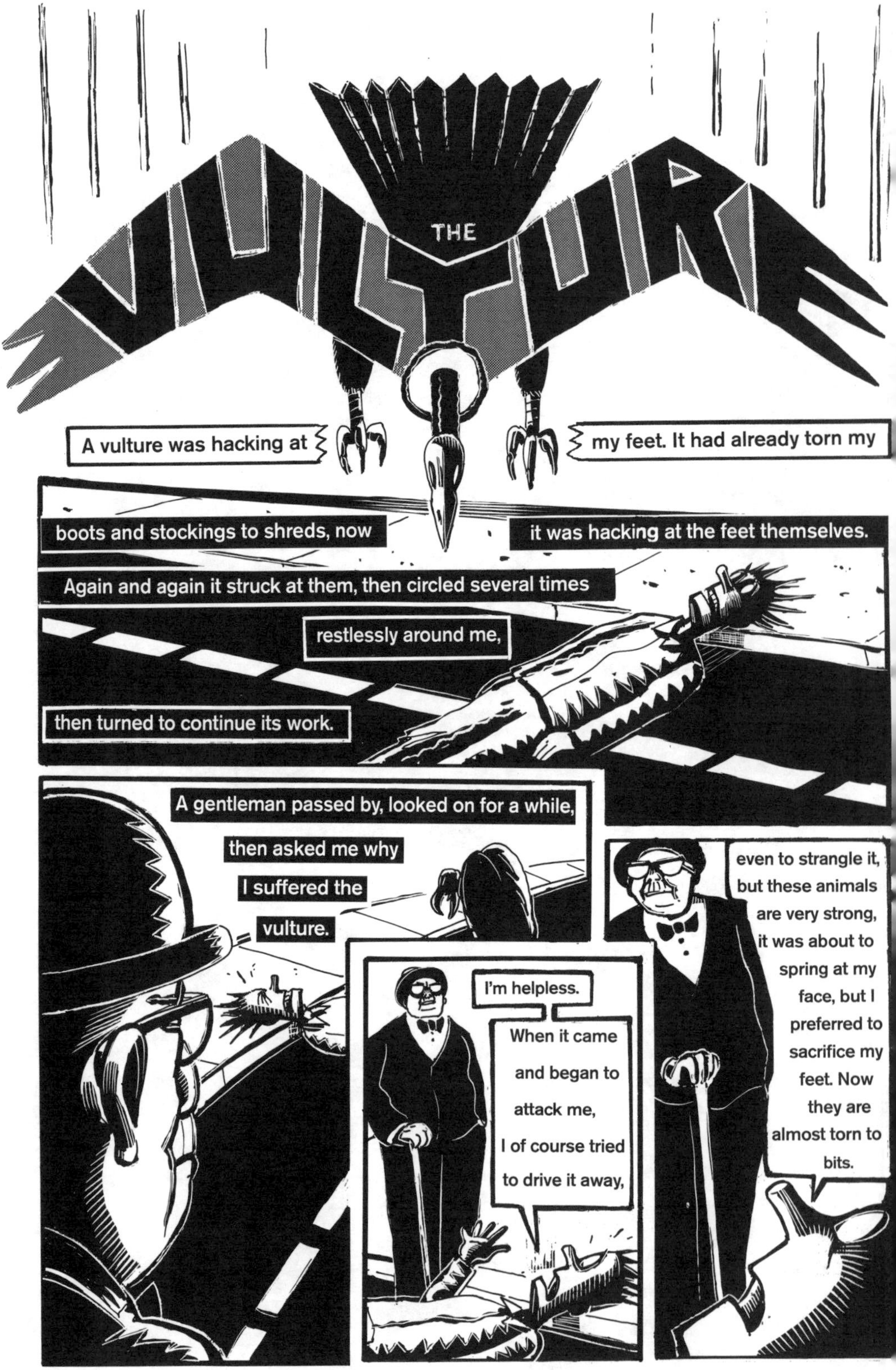
THE VULTURE
A vulture was hacking at
my feet. It had already torn my
boots and stockings to shreds, now
it was hacking at the feet themselves.
Again and again it struck at them, then circled several times
restlessly around me,
then turned to continue its work.
A gentleman passed by, looked on for a while,
then asked me why
I suffered the
vulture.
I'm helpless.
When it came and began to attack me, I of course tried to drive it away,
even to strangle it, but these animals are very strong, it was about to spring at my face, but I preferred to sacrifice my feet. Now they are almost torn to bits.

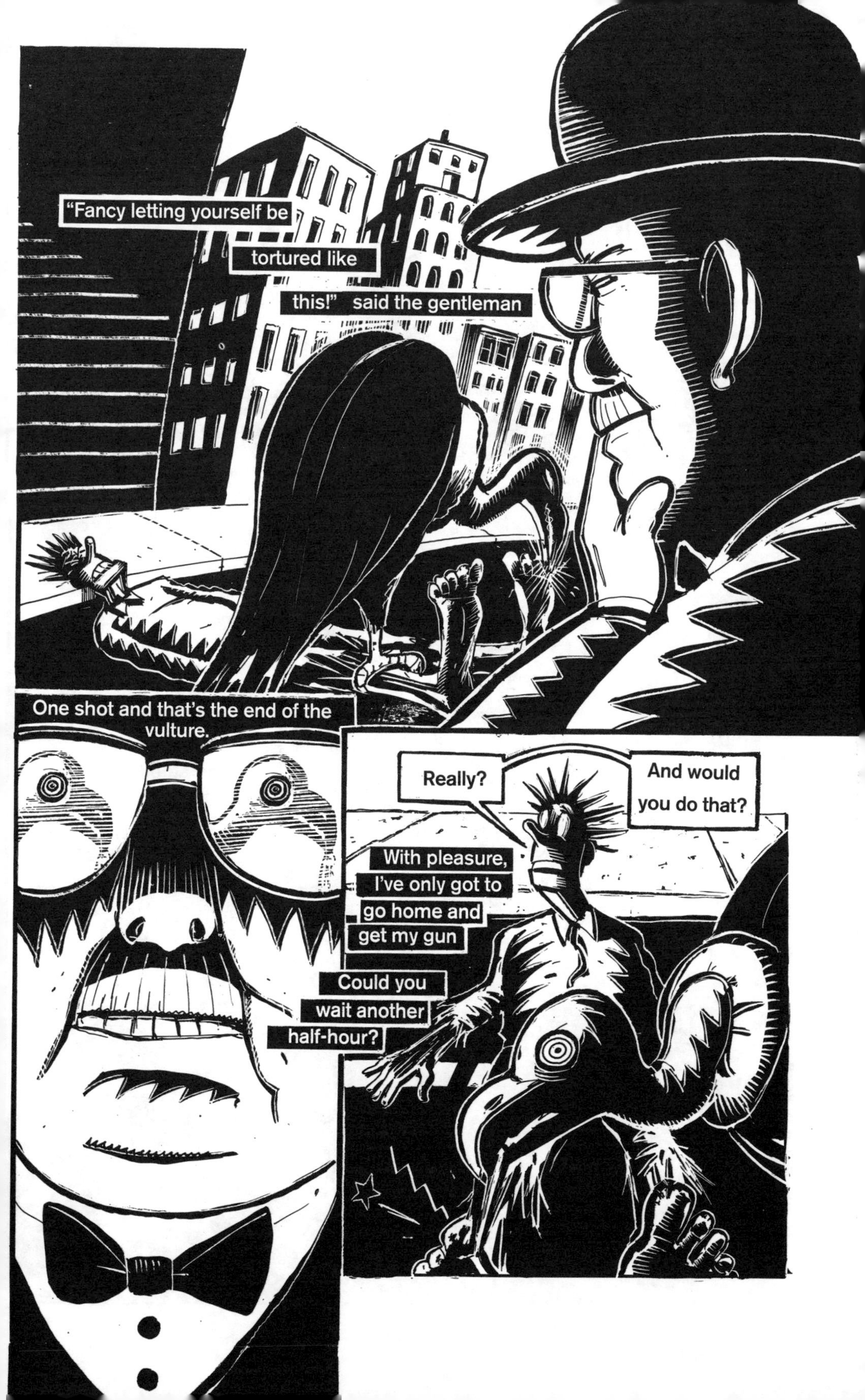

"Fancy letting yourself be
tortured like
this!" said the gentleman
One shot and that's the end of the vulture.
Really?
And would you do that?
With pleasure, I've only got to go home and get my gun
Could you wait another half-hour?

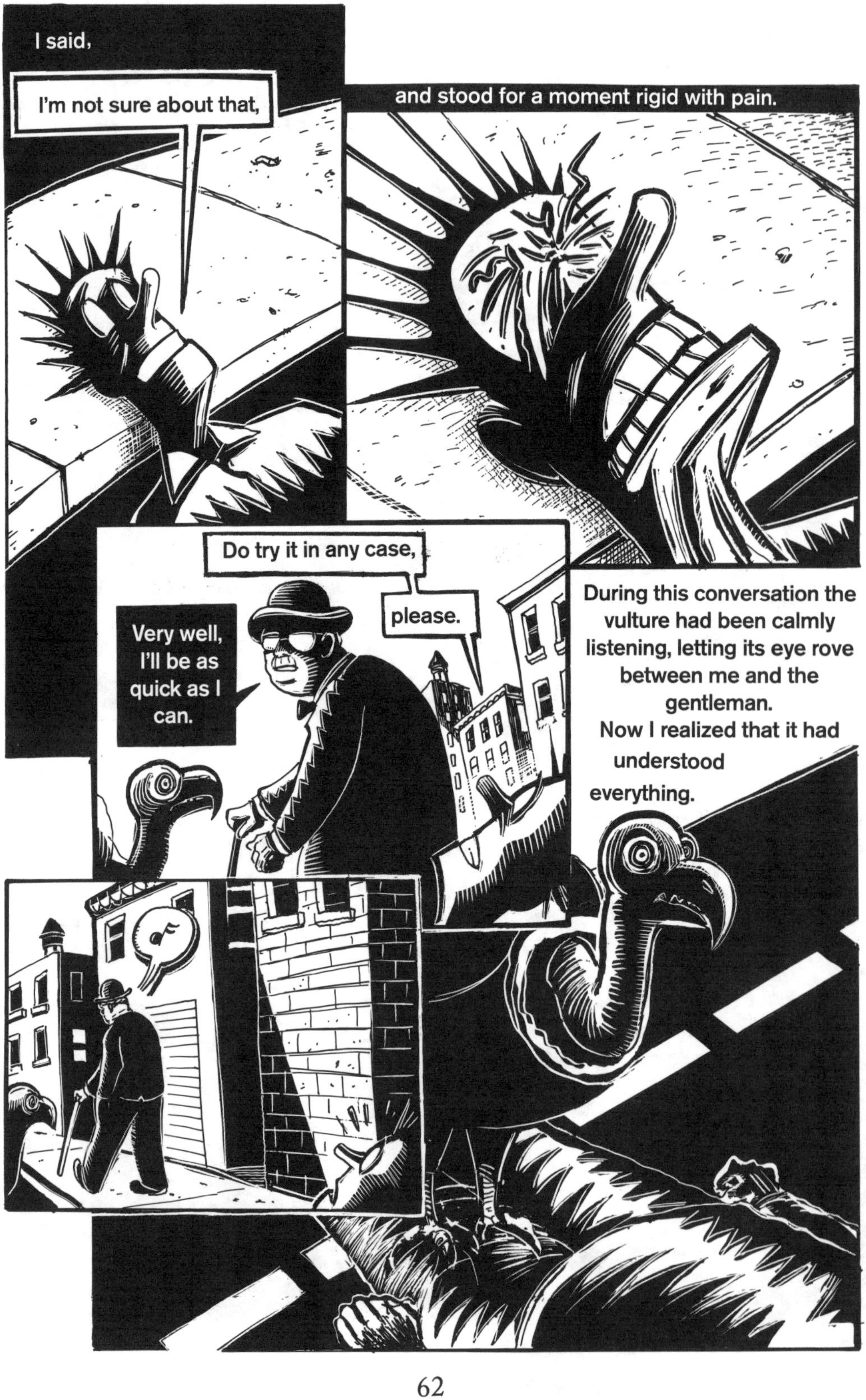
I said,
I'm not sure about that,
and stood for a moment rigid with pain.
Do try it in any case,
please.
Very well, I'll be as quick as I can.
During this conversation the vulture had been calmly listening, letting its eye rove between me and the gentleman.
Now I realized that it had understood everything.

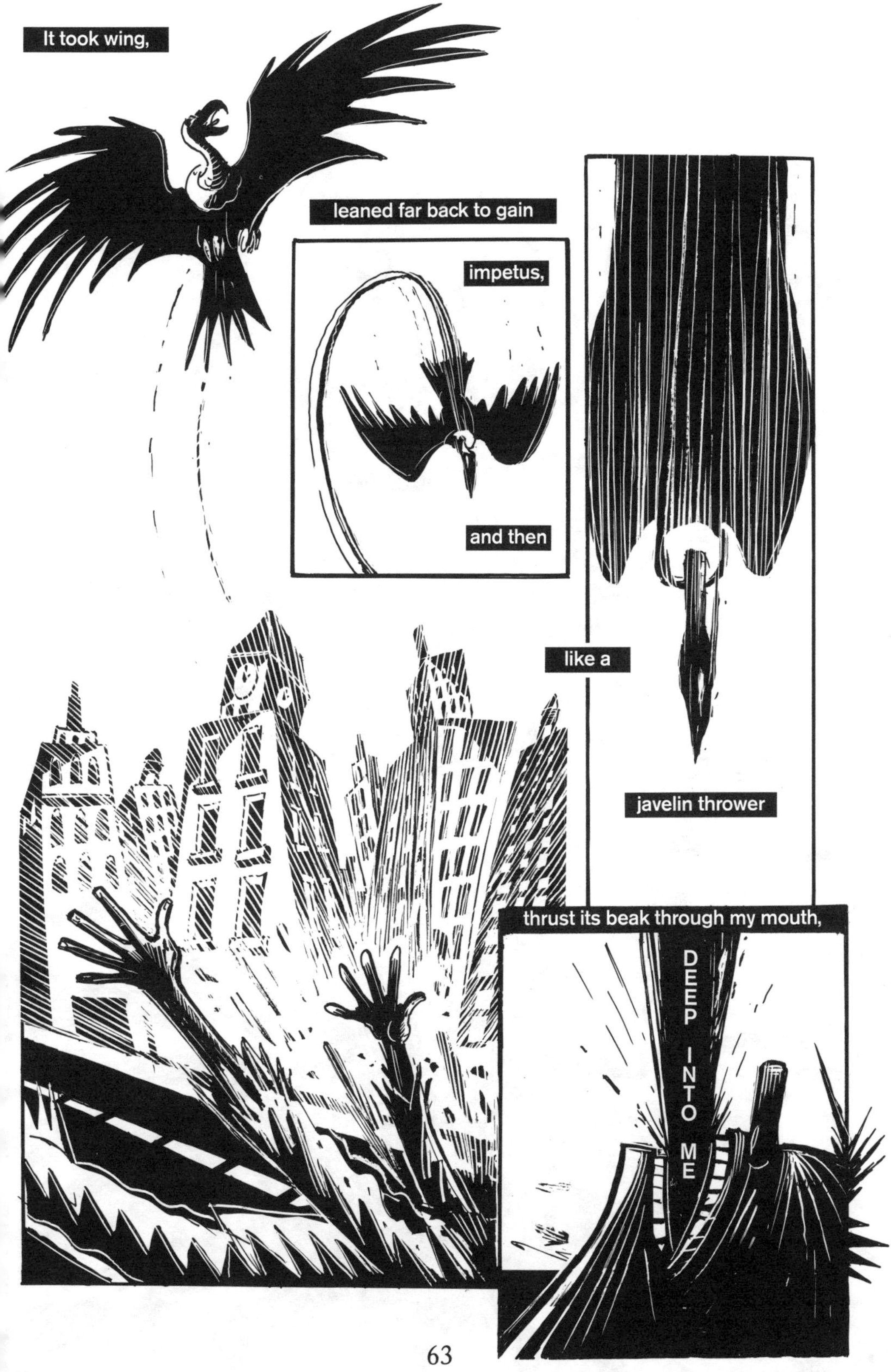
It took wing,
leaned far back to gain
impetus,
and then
like a
javelin thrower
thrust its beak through my mouth,
DEEP INTO ME

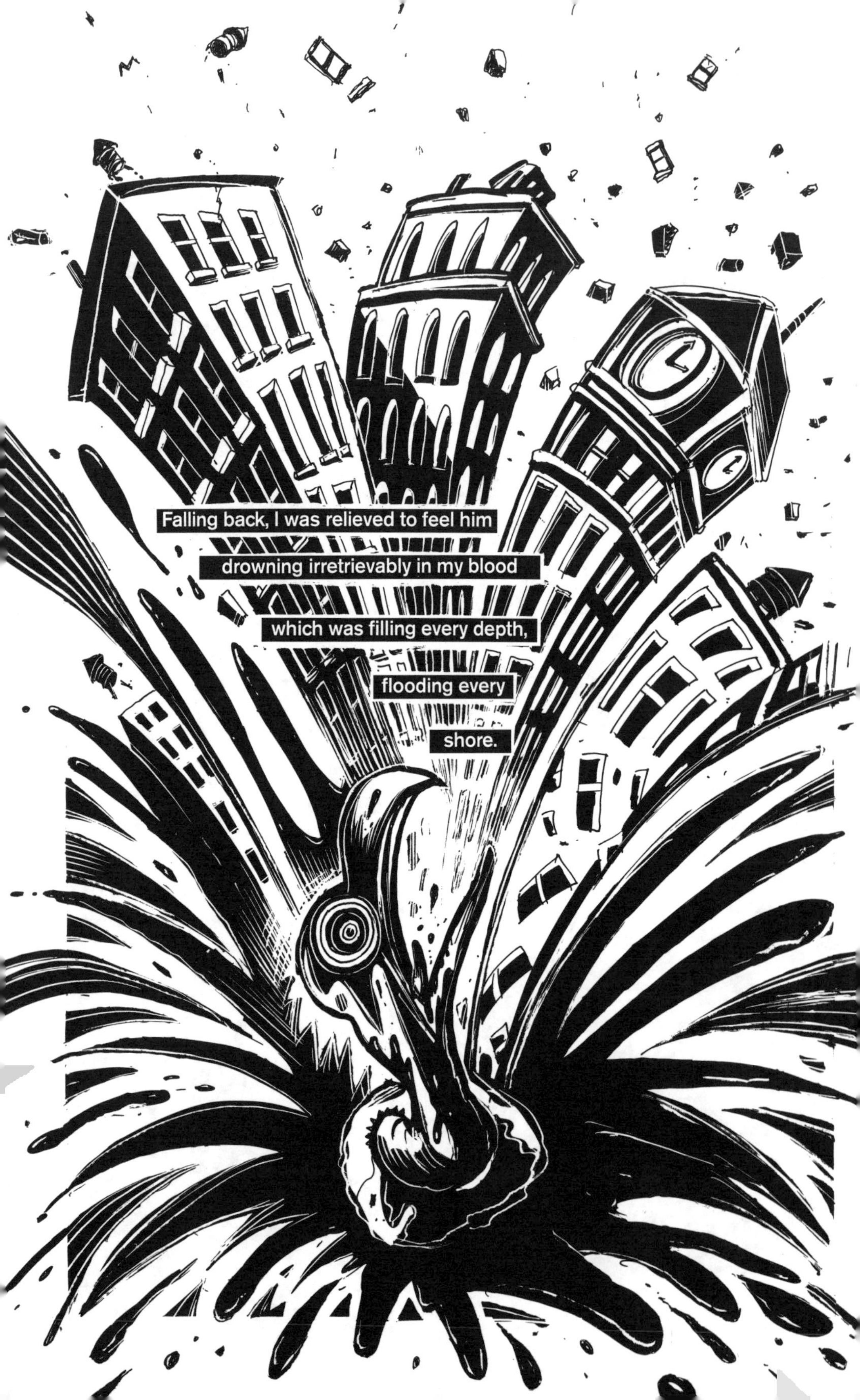
Falling back, I was relieved to feel him
drowning irretrievably in my blood
which was filling every depth,
flooding every
shore.